Also by James Mills

A NOVEL BY James Mills

ONE JUST MAN

SIMON AND SCHUSTER
New York

PUBLISHED BY SIMON AND SCHUSTER
ROCKEFELLER CENTER, 630 FIFTH AVENUE
NEW YORK, NEW YORK 10020

DESIGNED BY IRVING PERKINS
MANUFACTURED IN THE UNITED STATES OF AMERICA

1   2   3   4   5   6   7   8   9   10

LIBRARY OF CONGRESS CATALOGING IN PUBLICATION DATA

MILLS, JAMES, 1932-
ONE JUST MAN.

I. TITLE.
PZ4.M65570N   [PS3563.I423]   813'.5'4   74-18364
ISBN 0-671-21837-9

*No character in this book is meant
to portray a living person.*

ONE

A burning taxi was on its side in the intersection and when we slowed down to go around and get a look at it, I pushed open the door and jumped. I headed across Broadway and heard tires skid as Nicholson's foot hit the brake. Then footsteps, both men coming after me. I'd seen a familiar shape in the glow of the burning cab and I ran for it. Ajax, the albino, one arm missing.

When I got to him he yelled, "Come on, man," and led me on the run around the corner of 95th Street, up the block through a long alley, and then before Nicholson and Tacker could make the corner and spot us he had me in a doorway and we were taking steps two at a time. On the third floor we banged through a door into a loft and stopped. I stood panting my lungs out in bright lights and the heavy stink of sweat and gasoline and gunpowder.

A black man with a dirty white shirt torn up the back bent over a table covered with jewelry, money, identification papers, four or five pistols and a sawed-off shotgun. Under the table I saw women's handbags and a cab driver's coin changer and ten bottles filled with gasoline and rag fuses. The man quickly pulled a newspaper over what may or may not have been a submachine gun. The paper was *Right On!*, published by the Black Liberation Army. More of them, still tied with twine, were stacked next to the bottles.

Across the room two men sat in front of a TV set with the sound off, one of them nodding off to sleep, waking up, nodding off again.

Ajax caught his breath and grinned. "Hey, man, you really *did* it." He nodded toward the TV. "New York in flames, man."

"The TV says I did it?"

As I asked, my picture flashed on the screen. I was coming out of the Tombs in the middle of a crowd of prisoners and guards and soldiers. That had been two hours ago. The scene switched to Detroit and then to a studio in Washington.

I looked around the room. Someone with a Magic Marker had scrawled slogans on the walls. One was a familiar piece of Frantz Fanon's hysterical revolutionary rubbish. "And all the hopeless dregs of humanity, all who turn in circles between suicide and madness, march proudly in the great procession of the awakened nation." I thought of a couple of other quotes I could put on that wall, but I kept my mouth shut.

Ajax watched me read it. "The awakened nation, man. The nation is awake. They can't stop us now."

Ajax was insane. I usually like madmen, and I liked Ajax. He told the man at the table to put out the lights, and then he went to the window and untacked a blanket over it and looked out. "I don't see no one."

He moved away and I took a look. The street was deserted. The city was a war zone.

I stepped back.

"Law squad?" Ajax said.

"I don't think so. I think they're non-strikers. They picked me up outside the Tombs."

He was worried. "How hard they gonna look for you?"

I was afraid they'd look till they found me, but I didn't want to tell Ajax that. He wouldn't want anyone around drawing fire.

"They don't want me," I said, and moved over by the bottles of gasoline. "So what now?"

For a moment he didn't answer. Then, smiling: "Thanks. Thanks for gettin' us all out."

■

I had intended to tell this story straight through as fast as possible without stopping. But I had better speak quickly for a moment about my present situation, in case I am moved suddenly from this prison cell to an asylum. I have been expecting a visit from my attorney. I will send these pages out with him, whatever I have done by then. He is the one who must keep the authorities from moving me to a mental hospital.

It is five days since I jumped from the car on Broadway. I am in the administration isolation section of Attica State Prison, the only prison still intact in the State of New York. I was brought here two days ago from a general hospital in Stony Brook, New York, where I was treated for physical injuries you will hear more about later.

Administrative isolation is something close to solitary confinement. I am on a row with eleven cells, each occupied by a single inmate considered so dangerous, or so threatened, that he cannot be permitted contact with other inmates. Our cell doors may not be unlocked except in the presence of two guards armed with gas-filled steel clubs. For an hour each day, each of us is released alone into the barred corridor outside our cells. We can walk up and down and look in the other cells and talk to our fellow inmates. The rest of the time we can yell back and forth. Almost all the other inmates are insane. They pronounce isolation, ice-o-lation. They say they're on ice. We are all on ice.

I have a metal sign wired to my cell door. It says my name, Allan Dori, and beneath that, "HVP." High Violence Potential. Well, perhaps.

I am an enormous embarrassment to them here. I am charged with a variety of serious crimes, but they cannot try me. To begin with, they have at the moment no apparatus to try me. And in any case a trial would give me the opportunity to testify publicly about my motives and ideas. I would have finally the audience I lacked before. I would become almost certainly a martyr.

But to keep me here without trial, incognito, denying the news media access to me, is too embarrassing for them. So this morning they sent in the doctor. As soon as he asked me if I knew where I was, I saw what he was up to. In New York State a person can be legally committed against his will to a mental hospital on the word of only two doctors. They don't even have to be psychiatrists. Two obstetricians who say I'm crazy can send me away. That is my greatest fear. They want to lose me. They must lose me. They will try to shove me off into some psychiatric limbo beyond due process. I will never be heard from again.

Two years ago I was on a committee to examine laws regarding the mentally ill. I toured a state hospital for the criminally insane. I won't say what state or what hospital. On the floor where they kept—where they stored—

the most violent inmates, I saw taped to the wall a mimeographed notice. It informed inmates that they had the right to refuse electroshock treatments and lobotomy operations. I wondered how many involuntary treatments and operations must have been performed before that notice went up. And how many were still performed.

They used anectine there. Anectine is a drug employed against a patient after a particularly violent episode. It prevents proper breathing. The inmate thinks he's suffocating, drowning. He is filled with terror. The effect lasts about three minutes. During that time the doctor is saying, "The next time you feel violent, remember this sensation. Remember the pain and terror you feel now. Remember that when you are violent again you will feel this pain and terror again. Let that memory control your violence."

It's torture, of course. But they don't call it torture because it's done by doctors. And after all, the inmates *are* sick.

I will do anything I can to prevent their moving me to a hospital.

TWO

AJAX WAS frightening—blotched albino skin, white hair, prognathous jaw, arm stump uncovered, scarred, red. When he was four he watched a teenage brother rape his nine-year-old sister. When he was fourteen he came out of a state training school and hitchhiked west. In Nebraska he walked two days without a ride and finally planted himself in the middle of the road with his thumb out. A pickup truck took his arm off above the elbow. The cops found it two hundred yards up the road. The truck never stopped.

I'd known him since I took a thorn out of his paw two years ago. I got him time served for armed robbery and assault. He was nineteen, living on the street in Harlem, and he stabbed a sixty-year-old man in the neck, kicked him in the stomach and groin and took off with his wallet. When a cop grabbed him he said he got the wallet from the real robber and was running to the station house to turn it in. He sat in the Tombs ten months and then his case was called and I went down to the detention pen under the court to see him.

The Tombs was the medieval hole where Manhattan kept men awaiting trial who couldn't make bail. Ajax had

17

never been locked up before, and after ten months he was thin, filthy, scared and crazy, even crazier than usual. About thirty men were in the pen with him and I stood outside in that dirty yellow mens-room-tiled corridor and put my toe on a cross strip between the bars and balanced his file on my knee and tried to talk to him. He'd been too long between lawyers and he had a lot to say. I put my hand up and he stopped talking.

"Look, you can talk all you want to," I said. "But first there are some things I've got to know. So let me ask the questions first, and then you can talk all you want."

He nodded his head, very fast, anxious to get on with it.

"Now," I said starting out the same two-dollar speech I'd made a hundred thousand times before. "If you didn't do anything wrong, we're just wasting our time even talking about this. You'll go to trial."

That was as far as I got. He took hold of a bar with his hand and started yelling.

"Right, man. Right. I didn't do nothin' wrong. I don' even know why I'm here, man. I been here ten months. I told the lawyer ten months ago, I was just walkin' down the street and I saw this guy stab this old man and take his wallet and chased him and he dropped it and I picked it up and was runnin' to the police station with it and here come this cop and saw the old man lyin' there and me runnin'—me runnin', man—and he knocked me down just 'cause I was runnin' and I told him I was just takin' the wallet to the police to report everything, everything that happened, and they locked me up, man, they locked me up for savin' the old man's wallet. I been here ten months, man, I ain't never been in no jail before, I goin' crazy, man, I got to get out of here, if I don't get outa here I'm gonna kill myself, man, I'm gonna—"

I stopped him. Usually when they start talking about killing themselves it means they don't have anything more to say. It's their way of letting you know they've finished.

"Okay," I said. "It's very simple. If you're guilty of anything you can take the plea they've offered, which is a year, and under the circumstances that's a very good plea, and with your two months' good time you'll walk today. If you're innocent, then of course you'll go to trial."

His face twisted in concentration, that crazy, empty brain in there struggling to figure things out. "You mean if I take a plea I get out today, I walk today?"

"That's correct."

His file fell off my knee and I spent a little extra time picking up the papers and settling them back, letting him think things over. I didn't want problems.

"Okay, I take the plea. But I didn't do nothin', I didn't stab that man or nothin'."

Problems I was gonna have. "No. You don't understand. If you didn't do anything wrong, then you can't plead guilty. What kind of a system do you think we've got here? We wouldn't let an innocent man plead guilty. I wouldn't allow it and the DA wouldn't and the judge wouldn't."

"Well, I didn't do nothin' wrong. I ain't guilty."

Stubborn. And scared. Mostly scared. He was just smart enough to know he didn't know what was going on, and that scared him, as indeed it should have.

"Then you'll go to trial."

"When?"

"In a few months. Maybe longer."

Now it hit him. He couldn't believe it. I've seen this moment thousands of times and it always impresses me, the look of total shock on the faces of these little punks when they find out what kind of ridiculously evil ball game they're in.

"You mean," he said, this look of absolute unbelief working across his face, "you mean, if I'm guilty I get out today?"

"Right."

"And if I'm innocent I stay locked up?"

"You got it, man. So what are you gonna be, guilty or innocent?"

He turned around and walked back into the cell and slapped the wall with his hand and groaned, and then came back to the bars. "Man, I guess I'm guilty."

So they brought him upstairs and he pleaded guilty and the judge asked him what happened and he gave a blow-by-blow of how he stabbed and robbed the old man. No doubt at all that he did it. And he got his year and walked out and another case was off the calendar and another robber loose in the street. So the clerk called another name, a rapist this time, and I went back down in the pen to talk to him and give him a ten-minute crash course in the realities of our modern enlightened judicial structure.

I want to tell you I've been at the criminal lawyer business for a long time. I'm forty-five years old, I've been with New York's Legal Aid Society for seventeen years and I've represented something like seventy-five thousand indigent defendants. I've got an ego and I'm candid and it's the truth when I tell you I'm one of the five best criminal defense attorneys in New York. If you mistake that candor for conceit, you betray a preference for hypocrisy, and a hypocrite I'm not. I could have been a completely different kind of lawyer. In fact, for a short while I was a completely different kind of lawyer. Both my parents were lawyers. My father worked for the Duponts, and my mother was in a firm on Wall Street. I was twenty-one when they were driving back from Delaware and their limousine hit a truck on the turnpike. They left my sister and me seven million dollars. My sister never got her half. She was seventeen and she wrote a poem containing two lines of dialogue.

"Life is a nightmare you don't wake up from," he said.
"You do when you die," she said.

Nine weeks later she ingested the top three shelves of the medicine cabinet. She was cursed with the ability to feel—to feel to desperation, beyond endurance—that helps produce so many of our saints and suicides.

When I came out of law school I went in the Army. Then after the Army some friends of my parents got me a job on Wall Street. I spent six months writing wills for rich old ladies. The last day before my vacation I was leaving at three o'clock, getting an early start, and one of the partners stopped me in the hall and asked where I was going. I said on vacation. He said, No you're not, your vacation doesn't start till five-thirty, you're not leaving till five-thirty. I said, Well you are completely wrong. And I left and never went back and after vacation I joined the Legal Aid Society.

Something my father told me I have never forgotten, though I have rarely succeeded in living by it. He was spending a lot of time representing an old man who'd been thrown out by his landlord. He was the friend of our doorman or a maid or someone's chauffeur, I don't remember. Anyway, he was very poor, and had nothing whatsoever to do with the Duponts. I asked my father why he spent so much time on the case. He said, "He is as you are. He laughs, he cries, he fears, he dreams. So be kind. All you can do in life is be kind."

I never thought I was making a sacrifice by working for the Legal Aid Society when I could have been one of those talk-show lawyers with the big names and the rich clients. The other way around, it would have been a sacrifice. I was happy. I'll take a Puerto Rican purse snatcher to a rich old lady any day. My clients weren't Mafia bosses and bank embezzlers and suburban executives who'd shot their wives. I represented burglars, muggers, rapists, the people you meant when you talked about crime in the streets. My clients *were* crime in the streets.

And 98 per cent of them were guilty. So what? If that even interests you, you're on the wrong track. Friends of mine, non-lawyers, used to throw up their hands. How can you *say* that? Years ago I tried to explain it to my wife. I will tell you about my wife later. But I tried to explain it to her. We stood in the kitchen—me talking, her banging the pots and pans around. The defense attorney's not concerned with the community, I'd say. That's the DA's job. The defense attorney is concerned exclusively with the accused. Guilty men deserve representation as much as the innocent.

She'd bang the pots and not listen. Or pretend not to.

I was never overwhelmed with a feeling of social responsibility. At least not for the community as a whole—not unless I could see the responsibility in terms of individuals, individuals who were getting screwed. Like that situation Ajax the albino was in—if you're guilty you get out, if you're innocent you stay in. In Manhattan it got to the point where that sort of thing was happening a hundred times a day. The whole criminal justice structure—police, courts, jails—had become so clogged that only one arrest in thousands ever ended in a trial. Trials were obsolete. The presumption of innocence was dead. Defendants served their sentences before conviction. The government was saying to each defendant, "Look, if you'll abandon your unsupportable claim to innocence and save us the time and expense of a trial—for which anyway we don't *have* the time or money—we'll compensate you with a light sentence."

The defendant always said, "How light?" And then the haggling started. You could hear it not only in New York but in every criminal courthouse in every big city in America. It wasn't just, and it may not have been constitutional, but it worked for a while. They called it plea bargaining. The government needed guilty pleas to move cases out of court, and the defendants sold their guilty pleas for the only currency the government had to offer, which was time. But no matter what sentence was finally agreed on, the real outcome of the bargaining was never in doubt. The guilty always won. The innocent always lost.

The guilty got great deals. Six months for a heroin sale.

A year for armed robbery. Four years for murder. And the innocent? Well, there weren't that many of them. A handful. They were caged along with the others—raped, beaten, brutalized, driven to madness. They killed themselves and each other. And their lawyers stood and watched. The watchers were brutalized, too. Eventually, it was said, you became a stone, a lunatic, or a revolutionary. People used to say I was a stone. Now they'll tell you I'm all three.

I kept count of my suicides, clients of my own who used the knotted bedsheet. The number got up to 22. Then I did something. Can you imagine I waited so long? This story really begins with the one who tipped me over the edge. Alicia Bonner. She never really killed herself, never became the twenty-third. She was already dead the first time I talked to her.

One day in early summer, about two months ago, just a typical day. I got up, took a subway to the court building, bought a couple of Mars bars and a pack of Camels from the blind man in the lobby there and then went in the office. Peter Sonigo, this other attorney, was already there. We shared a dirty little office filled with a couple of old desks and files and stacked-up law books and newspapers, just off the big bullpen with the switchboard and clerks and some of the young lawyers.

Sonigo had a client sitting beside his desk, a huge young black guy with an Afro haircut with feathers sticking out of it. I threw the candy on my desk and nodded at Sonigo. The kid was on bail for robbery, going to court today, and Sonigo was giving him the doctor con.

"Look, kid, it's like this. If you're innocent you should go to trial, if you're guilty maybe you should tell me and we can think of what to do. You know, if you're sick and you've got a pain in the head and you tell the doctor you've got a pain in the leg, then—"

The kid sat back in the chair. "I'm innocent."

"Okay. Fine. So we'll go to trial. But if at some later date you should happen to become a little guilty, you let me know, okay?"

The guy left.

"He'll never go to trial and you know it," I said.

"I guess you're right. Man, that's the whole act, ain't it? Get up the bail and out of jail and they never get around to you."

He was too fat, and he sweated a lot. He was sweating now. He coughed and spat into the wastebasket and poked around for his coffee cup in the piles of papers on his desk. "I don't know what's the matter with me. I'm sick all the time."

"Tuberculosis." We'd worked together for thirteen years.

"Better than that wasting-away terminal disease you've got. Thinner and thinner and thinner."

He went into the bullpen for coffee, and I looked through the files of my day's menu. Forty cases, mostly robberies and burglaries. A couple of rapes, attempted homicides, a forgery. Susan Bernfeld came in wanting to fill me in on a case of hers I might have to handle. She'd only been with us a couple of weeks but I thought I had her pegged. A familiar type. Fresh out of St. John's, twenty-three-year-old romantic, still thought the criminal

25

courts were an arena where you could battle evil for the rights of mankind. Wonderful. Believed everything. Very *careful* to believe everything, just to insure that no truth be turned away.

She was maybe a touch too heavy, with short brown hair and New York skin. But she had nice breasts. And she had a very pretty face—high, delicate, assertive cheekbones, a nose too perfect to be the work of any surgeon, and huge, sparkling blue eyes.

"Alicia Bonner's on the calendar in Part Seven," she said. "I'm assigned to Part Three so I may not be able to get there. She's been in ten months—a single drug sale— and she says she's innocent."

She looked at me and blinked.

"Don't smile like that," she said. "This one *is* innocent. She's a nineteen-year-old runaway from Chester, Iowa. The sale was made, but she didn't make it. Her pimp was dealing and they got busted together in a hallway with a junkie who said she sold to him. He was afraid of the pimp."

"I'll talk to her," I said. "Of course I know she's innocent and she ought to go to trial and remove this unjust and ugly stain from her previously unblemished reputation. But just in case she's offered time served what would you say?"

"I'd say she's innocent and she shouldn't have to plead guilty just so she can get out. And you shouldn't be so cynical."

"My dear, if cynicism can get your client on the street, and sentimentality keeps her in, you ought to give cynicism some very serious thought."

"What about Alicia?"

"All I can do is explain the rules to her. If I can get her a good deal and she wants to plead, that's her business. How about lunch?"

She walked out. She had grown up in a near-poverty home with eight brothers and sisters, a mother who worked and a father who drank. But there had been protection. She would learn things from the defendants.

I went upstairs to Part Seven, Judge Joseph Bianchi. Bianchi was one of the most corrupt judges in New York County but more effective and competent than any of the others. He just had his own very special idea about the law. Not about the law, really, but about the way it was practiced at the moment. I really shouldn't have said he was corrupt. He had simply accommodated himself logically and rationally to a perverted system. He figured as long as the government was plea bargaining, he might as well do a little private, free-enterprise bargaining on his own. Nothing too destructive, you know. I mean if some lunatic who slaughtered seven people with an ax wanted a walk—well, he couldn't buy it from Bianchi. The man had principles. But maybe you need a little bail reduction? A sentence vacated?

I've got some money myself, as I said, and from time to time I've done business with Bianchi in the interest of a client. Why not? If the rich have corruption, the poor should have it too. I figure some guinea hoodlum with Mafia money can buy a break, why not some poor junkie burglar too dumb to know how to steal? It's supposed to be an impartial system.

I liked working with Bianchi. He was smart, fast and efficient. No bullshit. Which may be why the Appellate Division hadn't been too fast to come down on him for some of his suspiciously mild sentences. More than any-thing else in this world, the AD needed judges who moved cases, who didn't postpone half of them and shove them onto someone else's calendar.

When I walked into court the Assistant DA was already there, laying out files on the counsel table.

"How's the garden?" he said.

"Dead. And high time, too." I raise tulips and vege-tables on a little weekend farm upstate.

I was happy to see I had Fischer. He was a good ADA. Young like most of the others, about twenty-eight, and black—mod, Afro haircut. And funny, an amusing wit, sharp, nice to have around late in the day when you're tired. He carried a picture around in his wallet of what he looked like when he joined the DA's office. Short wavy hair. "Like a Negro shoe salesman," he said. "Now look at me, man. A black DA." His father had been a judge, shot and killed by holdup men running out of a liquor store in Harlem. His sister married an FBI man. Fischer was just putting in time as an ADA before he went into politics.

"What are we gonna do with Bedford?" he said, looking at a file. We were the only ones in the courtroom.

"That's not mine." I said.

"Yes it is, Al. Don't bullshit me. Take a look."

I sat down in the jury box and spread the cases out on the rail. I picked up Bedford. Robbery with a knife. Multiple stab wounds. Last time in court the DA offered a Class E felony with a top of three years. I figured I'd see how good a mood Fischer was in. "This isn't worth three years, David. People get three years for homicide."

"Will you take a bullet?"

A bullet's a year. I knew it was going to be a good day. "Bianchi won't go for that," I said.

Fischer sat down at the counsel table and stretched and yawned. "So we'll give it to him someplace else. We'll help him. We'll give him a helping judge."

The DA's office assigns cases to judges. If they wanted to move this one to someone else they could do it.

"Okay with me," I said.

"I thought it would be."

The clerks arrived and then the judge. We got going. After the first few cases I found out how good Fischer's mood really was. A black boy tried to stick up a bakeshop by pretending to have a gun in his jacket pocket. Up at the bench, Fischer said to me and the judge, "He's only twenty and the gun was simulated and he's only got two prior arrests so—" he looked up at the clock—"this is my eleven-thirty special. Grab it while it's hot. An E and a flat." A flat is a year.

Bianchi looked at me. "I'd grab that fast, Al."

"Consider it grabbed. Bring him in."

He came in and sat down at the defense table and I whispered the offer to him. "They're offering an E and a bullet."

He'd been in four months. He said he wanted time served. I told him that would never happen. "You'll never get a plea like this offered again. It's one of the best I've ever heard."

The judge was reading *The New York Times*. Fischer sat at his table ten feet away, waiting.

"But I ain't never been arrested before."

"You've got two previous."

"That was petty larceny."

"Petty larceny counts, too. If you want to be a wise guy you've got a perfect right. But this is the best offer you'll get and you probably won't get it again. So you want to go to trial?"

Dumb kid. He'd sit in the Tombs another week or two and then they'd bring him back and by then he'd have changed his mind, but Fischer would be in a different mood or it'd be a different ADA altogether and the offer would be up to three years.

Fischer smelled it. He walked by the table. "He doesn't *want* it?"

The boy looked up at him. He and Fischer were the only black men in the room. "Who's he?"

"Don't have nothin' to do with me, man," Fischer said. "I'm the enemy."

He walked away a couple of steps and then turned back. "Don't mark that down as an offer, Al. The offer is withdrawn in two minutes."

"He says, and rightly so, that he's never had a felony arrest before," I said to Bianchi. "And the gun was simulated—"

The kid nodded.

Fischer saw the nod. "He admits it. He *admits* it—and he won't take the plea. What do these guys want from us?"

I turned back to the boy. "You sure you want to go to trial? If you're convicted you could get fifteen years. You know you're guilty."

"I'm guilty. But I want time served. I don't want no year."

I looked at the judge. "Ready for trial, your honor."

And they took him out. A failure. If he'd taken the plea he'd have moved tomorrow to a prison upstate. Now he'd go back to the Tombs and he'd be back here and then back to the Tombs again and back and forth till he took a plea. Clogging up the system.

After the dumb kid we got a lunatic accused of stabbing to death an old lady who lived across the hall. She borrowed his radio and wouldn't give it back. Down in the pen he told me a burglar stabbed her. He said the police arrested him because they found a steak knife in his kitchen. He said he didn't understand pleas, didn't understand guilt or innocence, he just knew he was there because the cops found his steak knife.

"Your honor," I said, "the only thing the defendant will plead guilty to is possession of a steak knife. You can take that if you want, but I don't think it's in the penal code."

"He carried a *steak* knife?"

"One can't always afford the knife of one's choice, your honor."

"A *sirloin* steak knife?"

"Sirloin or chuck. I didn't ask."

The case was marked "Ready," and we forged ahead.

It was getting close to noon, and hotter than hell. That courtroom was oppressive at any time, and in summer it could make you wish you were dead. Dim light, high ceiling, rows and rows of brown church-pew seats. About thirty people were there that day—cops, defendants on bail, fat big-bosomed mothers fanning themselves with folded copies of *El Diario*. And complainants, mostly com-

31

plainants, almost all of them first timers. Once you'd been through the aggravation and harassment of multiple court appearances you learned to nurse your wounds at home and forget about retribution. The recidivism rate among complainants was very low.

The judge wanted to give two years to a man who shot and killed his wife. The man had never been in trouble before. Fischer was outraged.

"I won't do it, your honor. This is abominable. Some guy wants to get rid of his wife so he just blows her head off. That girl had a large family—sisters, brothers. She was only twenty-four. I can't do it. Two years. For murder. No, your honor, I can't. It's disgusting."

"It disgusts me, too," Bianchi said with a little heat. "I wouldn't even suggest it if it weren't for the crowded conditions in our courts."

"Your honor, we've been giving away the courthouse because of the conditions, and this is too much. No."

He stepped back to his table. "The people are ready for trial, your honor."

I walked past him and he said to me, "Is that unreasonable, Al? Tell me."

He was very distraught. I felt sorry for him. "No, Dave. I don't think it is."

Bianchi didn't say anything. He was waiting. The Presiding Justices of the Appelate Division were all over him to move cases, and he knew the DA was telling assistants like Fischer not to obstruct, that cases had to be moved. But this was pushing Fischer's limits.

He stood by the table, shoving folders around. "Your honor, if he takes it right this *second*—"

So the man got two years for murdering his wife.

I was sitting in the jury box. Fischer came over and leaned across the railing. "What do I do? What do I tell the father and mother when they call and want to know what happened to the man who murdered their daughter?"

I had lunch with Susan. We went to Carlo's, a place behind the court building filled with lawyers and cops and judges and correction officers from the Tombs. It was so crowded they had to set two places for us at the bar. I told her Alicia Bonner's case hadn't been called yet.

"I'm sorry I said you were cynical," she said. We'd been on the subject once before—my cynicism versus her innocence—and had called a truce.

"Forget it," I said. "I consider it a compliment. I've been called a cynic so many times I don't even deny it to myself anymore. And what's wrong with cynicism? It's had a bad press. Cynicism's just a love of mankind as it really is, not as some fools and cowards say it is. Love without the sentimentality. And to be a cynic one must first have been an idealist. Remember that."

"So you're a failed idealist."

"Well, maybe not completely failed. Don't make me worse than I am."

"A compassionate cynic."

"I'll accept that."

"I think you're an act, the cynicism's a defense."

"Against what?"

"People."

"Well, perhaps. But if it is an act, it's a very carefully cultivated one. If you look like a ruthless, cynical bastard to the ADAs they get scared and the offers come down. Myths are very important in this business."

We were having spaghetti and clam sauce. She listened and didn't say much. I wondered if her silence was timidity. I'd heard that one of her older brothers fired a shot at her father when he came home drunk and started beating up on the wife and kids. Or maybe she was smart enough to lie back silent, soaking it all up, going to school on other people's brains. Mine, for example.

"You really think they're all guilty?" she said.

"Not all. Maybe one or two percent are mistaken-identity cases or police frames. But most. The presumption of innocence is the most faulty presumption ever made. Ask the other lawyers who've been around awhile. I couldn't tell you for sure that I've ever defended an innocent man."

"You're kidding." She looked surprised. They don't talk to you like that in law school.

"Not at all. Innocence is much harder to know than guilt. And anyway, what difference does it make? I'd much rather defend a guilty man. Then if you lose—well, so what? And if you win! Wow! What a triumph. You convinced twelve men that what was true was not true. And you did it over the skilled, talented, strenuous efforts of the New York City Police Department and the District Attorney's office. Fantastic. Much more satisfying than defending an innocent man. He *is* innocent, so any idiot lawyer ought to be able to prevent someone from proving he's guilty. All the facts are on your side. The truth is on your side. But defending the guilty—that can be very satisfying."

"You have some ego," she said.

34

"Even my ego has an ego."

She stopped chewing and blinked. You had to *see* those eyes. "But if he's guilty, let's say he raped a child or something, and he gets turned loose, then he's your responsibility. If he does it again, you're the one—"

"No, no, no. What did they teach you in law school anyway? He's society's responsibility, the system's. I didn't invent the criminal justice system. The system doesn't say anything about if he's guilty or not. It says can he be *proved* guilty. And if he can't, so be it. Listen, if he goes out and rapes another child and gets caught I'll defend him just as vigorously a second time, and a third and a fourth. Not for him. For the system."

"And for your ego."

"It doesn't matter. It's still right. If you don't feel that way you shouldn't practice. It's the greatest judicial system ever developed."

"If it's so great how come it's so fucked up?"

"Dirty talk. And such a pretty girl. You're getting cynical already."

"Answer me."

"When I get it figured out I'll let you know."

I had another visit from a doctor today, a different one this time, a psychiatrist. He tried to talk me into moving voluntarily to a hospital. That's a good sign. They don't want to commit me involuntarily. I told him he was crazy for even asking.

"Why not?" he said. "Why don't you want to go?"

I am not accurately reporting his speech. He has a stutter. I will leave the stutter out. He is a tall, skinny, cadaverous man, his face as white as his jacket.

"I don't want to go because I'm not crazy. And because I don't think being crazy has anything to do with your wanting me to go. If you want to hospitalize a crazy man, then take one of my fellow inmates here. They are all nutty as bedbugs. The one in the first cell sits all day in the corner chirping like a bird. The one next door told me if I come within reach he'll pull my arms off and eat them. If you don't take them, why me? I'm not crazy. What makes you so convinced I'm crazy?"

"Well, you sound awfully determined to stay in prison. Most normal people would rather be in a hospital than in a prison."

"So as long as I protest that I'm sane and want to stay

here instead of in an asylum you say I'm mad and ought to be in the asylum?"

"More or less."

"And if I admit that I'm mad, I'll go to the asylum also?"

"Of course."

"So either way, I'm mad and ought to go to the asylum."

"You're twisting my words."

No word yet from my attorney.

THREE

I<small>N COURT</small> that afternoon, after lunch with Susan, I was going through a file, getting ready to talk about a robbery case, when I heard the judge say to Fischer, "Attempt robbery three, and leave the driving to me."

"You're a poet, Judge," Fischer said.

"What is it?" I asked Fischer.

"Tried to stick up a cab. Torres."

I flipped through my cases and pulled out Torres and looked at it.

"I haven't seen him yet, your honor," I said.

"Leave it to me, Al," Bianchi said. "It'll be an easy one. Bring him up."

"But I haven't even interviewed him. I haven't seen him."

"Time served, Al. He'll snap at it. We've got ten more cases waiting. You don't need to interview him. Bring him up."

So I walked out to the hall between the courtroom door and the pen stairs and waited for him to come up. It's not even a hall, really, just a small space about five feet square. The walls are yellow tile, the brown floor covered with cigarette butts dropped by waiting defendants and guards.

The gate clanged open below and a Puerto Rican with a week's beard came to the top of the stairs.

I said, "They're offering time served, Torres. You can't get any less than that. It's a walk, out today, so—"

"Mr. Dori," the guard said, "this isn't Torres. It's Perez. Torres'll be up in a second. They're getting him from one of the other pens."

I walked back into court and sat down in the jury box and didn't say a word. Torres in effect had been tried, convicted, and sentenced in three minutes flat, and without his attorney even knowing what he looked like. And he'd already served his sentence, served it before he even pleaded.

"What's wrong, Al? Something the matter?"

It was Fischer.

"No, Dave. Nothing. They'll have him up in a minute. Perez is out there now. You want to take him while we wait? It's two sales of heroin."

"Easy," said Fischer. "An E and a bullet on each."

So Perez went for two times an E and a bullet, and then Torres went for time served, which was six months, and by the time they called Alicia Bonner I had just about had it. You know, your juices come back overnight, and you have time to rationalize and make speeches and excuses to yourself. But late in the day, those last couple of hours, it gets hard to swallow.

I talked to Alicia in that stinking little hallway above the stairs. It had started to rain, a thunderstorm. It was dark out and windy. A casement window, opaque with chicken wire between the plates, had been cracked open, and damp cold air and rain were blowing in and making things even more miserable for Alicia. I tried to close the window but it was jammed. She seemed not to care or notice. She was a junkie—wire-thin, with deep, lost, wandering eyes, and a face sad and dead, as if all the muscles that could make it laugh or frown or show fear or anger had been cut. She stood there shivering in a dirty orange T-shirt, no socks, no shoelaces, the backs of her sneakers pushed in like slippers, her hands stiff-armed down into the pockets of beltless jeans with a broken zipper. Very quietly, she told me she was innocent.

"Well, if you are then you'll have to go to trial."

"Yes. That's what I want."

Her voice was so low I had to lean close to hear her. I took out her interview and read it.

"You say your friend Hank made the sale, but the guy buying fingered you because he was afraid of Hank."

"That's right."

"I beg your pardon?"

"That's right."

Her eyes started to wander around the hall, and she was no longer with me. I waited two minutes and she said nothing, didn't look at me, just stood there like a zombie. I felt a sudden urge and touched her face. Her eyes came back to me. I looked again in her folder. She'd been in ten months. She'd been examined at Bellevue and returned to the Women's House of Detention as legally sane.

"Well, Alicia . . ."

She looked at me.

"Alicia, I think that if you are guilty of anything, anything at all, I can get you time served. That means you'll get out today."

43

"Yes. That's what I want."

She seemed about to say something else so I kept quiet.

"I don't want to go back to him."

"You won't have to. Hank's in jail."

"I mean Mike."

"Who's Mike?"

"This black butch in the House. He says he's gonna give me to the other dykes. I'll kill myself."

"Well, you don't have to go back, if you're guilty of anything. Maybe you didn't make the sale, but maybe you were just carrying the weight for your friend. If you had something on you I can get it reduced to possession and you can plead to that and get out."

"I want to get out."

"I'll see what I can do."

I went back to court and explained the situation to Bianchi and Fischer and they agreed to go for time served. A guard brought her up and she stood before the bench. She was in a daze.

I made my little speech for the record about the defendant now wishing to withdraw her original plea of not guilty, made some months ago, and plead guilty to the third count of the indictment, possession, that plea to cover the entire indictment.

Fischer got up, bored and routine, reciting the words very fast as he read the next case. "Your honor, the people respectfully recommend acceptance of this plea, feeling that it will provide the court with adequate scope for punishment in the interest of justice."

Bianchi looked at Alicia. She was in another world.

"Miss Bonner, at the time and place stated in the indictment, were you in fact in possession of three seven-dollar bags of heroin?"

She shook her head and whispered.

"I can't hear her. What did she say?"

I'd heard her. She'd said no.

"Excuse me, your honor," I said. I whispered to her, "You can't get out, you can't plead guilty, unless you admit it, you'll have to go to trial."

She stared at me.

"That will be months from now. And probably you'll be convicted."

She kept staring. I didn't know if she even heard me.

"Do you want to get out today?" I asked her.

"Yes. I don't want to go back."

"Then when the judge asks if you were in possession you'll have to give the appropriate answer."

I looked up at Bianchi. He tried again. "Miss Bonner, were you in possession of this heroin, the heroin mentioned in this indictment?"

She shook her head.

The stenographer, his head twisted toward her, said, "I can't hear her, your honor."

"I can't either," Bianchi said. "You'll have to speak up, Miss Bonner. We have to be able to hear you. What is your answer?"

She shook her head. "I didn't have it. Hank—"

"You want a second call, Al?" Bianchi said.

"Yes, your honor."

The guard stepped up to take her out. When his hand touched her elbow, her face suddenly contorted. She screamed and dropped to the floor. I leaned over her. She

45

was sobbing. "It's all right, Alicia. They're not taking you back. I just want to talk to you some more outside. It's all right."

A matron arrived and helped her out.

Ten minutes later Alicia had calmed down and we were back in the hallway. I explained things to her again. She said she didn't want to go back to the dykes. But she wouldn't say she had done anything wrong. She was innocent, or thought she was, and she was so obsessed by her belief in her innocence that she was incapable of denying it. I think she was incapable of even understanding the necessity of denying it. Of course she was insane, but Bellevue had said she was not insane, so that left the problem with me. For half an hour I tried to make her understand that she had to admit possessing the heroin. She kept repeating that she didn't have it, Hank had it. How can you fight that? All she could see was the truth, or what she believed to be the truth. She didn't have it. Hank had it. Period.

So she didn't plead, and she didn't get the walk. It took three matrons to get her back down the stairs. She was screaming.

I tried to stay away from Susan after court, but before I could leave she was standing by my desk. She didn't say anything, she just stood there and glared. Sonigo brushed past her on his way out and I closed the door behind him. We were alone.

"You heard," I said.

She was silent.

"Well, sit down, anyway."

She sat down.

"Susan, I'm sorry. There was nothing I could do. I tried

as hard as I could. Bianchi and Fischer and I wanted her out of there as much as you do. But what the hell could we do? She wouldn't even admit possession."

"Did you tell her to admit possession?"

"Damned near."

"Did you?"

"Of course not. I'm not going to tell someone who's innocent, or might be, to say they're guilty. What the hell do you think I am? And this is some change of heart for you. You're the one who said innocent people shouldn't have to plead guilty."

She was beginning to annoy me. She was cute, sexy, probably fairly bright, and I liked her. But I didn't need her telling me how to handle cases. I felt bad enough as it was.

"I think you're someone who made that pathetic creature go back into hell so you wouldn't have to violate your precious concern for a lot of ethical horseshit."

"Ethical horseshit. Very nice. And you're supposed to be a lawyer."

"Alicia Bonner is supposed to be a human being. What do you want, legality or justice?"

"I thought maybe they were the same thing."

"Justice can be illegal."

"Sometimes. Then you have to choose between the law and chaos."

"You care about Alicia as a legal curiosity. Interesting legal problem. Now how do we attorneys cope with this interesting little judicial problem here?"

"And you care about her as a human being, right? And fuck the law."

"Right."

"You shouldn't be here," I said. "You shouldn't have stayed in law school, and you sure as hell shouldn't be in a criminal court."

"I believe you. I should be somewhere with a bomb."

"With a bomb. Oh, fine. That's a great way to show your regard for the individual. Blow the bastards up." I laughed. "I'll bet you've got a poster of Che Guevara in your living room."

"I don't have a living room. It's over the bed."

"How lucky for him."

"And what did you put on your walls? When you were young."

"Model airplanes."

"I believe it."

"You're too sentimental to be a revolutionary. The Guevaras and Maos, they're thugs who read. You don't have the cruelty. You've got to pull the trigger smiling, quoting poetry. You couldn't do that. You'd better marry some Maoist history professor and stay home and have babies."

Sonigo had a two-inch-high bronze ashtray on his desk, cut off from a navy shell casing, solid and heavy. She reached back and picked it up and held it in the palm of her hand.

"You want to be tough," I said. "You mistake toughness for experience and knowledge."

"What would you know about toughness?" Her blue eyes were cold and challenging, the voice brittle. "Rich people think because they're mean they're tough. If someone came in here with a bomb and said come with us we're going to get the Alicias out, I'd go."

"You'd better put the ashtray down."

She put it down and left. I was amazed and angry. I sat at my desk for thirty minutes thinking about her, and trying to think up things I should have said. Then I took a subway home, and kept on thinking. I couldn't get Susan out of my mind, and I couldn't come up with any satisfying rationale that would let me get rid of Alicia, either. None of the old arguments worked—they were overused, exhausted. I'd never known anyone with more faith in the system than she had. She believed she was innocent, and she believed her innocence was a fact as absolute and undeniable as the moment of her birth. Only madmen pleaded innocent. I kept hearing her sobs and cries as she was taken back to jail. I heard the sobs and cries of the past seventeen years.

Susan came into my office at noon the next day and said she was sorry for what had happened. I told her it was okay, I was sorry too, we all had things to learn from each other, and how about lunch. We went to Carlo's, and she pushed her emotions back down to where she usually kept them.

Sonigo and his wife had asked me to dinner that night at their apartment on the lower East Side. It was the first time in six months I'd been to anything resembling a party. I took Susan with me, partly because I thought she might learn something, partly as protection from Helen Sonigo, and partly because I was trying to get her into bed.

Peter took about three minutes unfastening a half-dozen locks, then pulled the door open, stepped back, and tripped over a table. The room was small and completely filled with chairs, tables, lamps, hassocks, a grandfather clock, and plants. Plants came at you from everywhere—tables, windowsills, bookshelves, the floor. Windows were closed. The heat was stifling. Everything looked the work of Helen, except for a sailfish Peter had taken off the Florida keys when he was twenty-four. The sailfish was mounted with a brass plaque over the fireplace.

Helen appeared from the kitchen in black tights and a blouse, weaving expertly towards us through the foliage and furniture. Peter maneuvered cautiously into a small clearing in the center of the room, reached under a table and came up with a Jack Daniel bottle and a shot glass. For the rest of the evening he never let go of either. He sat with the bottle between his legs, and when he moved he took the bottle with him. If you wanted the bottle you had to hit him from behind.

"Really, Pete," Helen said. "Why do you bother to lug the glass around? Why don't you just drink out of the bottle?"

He didn't answer. He just gave this deep-throated, phlegmy laugh, then coughed, then sat down on a sofa next to Susan. He looked at her, about to say something, and she blinked at him and moved her shoulders. He turned back eyes front and looked stunned, trying to think what it was he'd been about to say. She was wearing tight white pants and a yellow blouse with no bra.

Peter hadn't told me Jeff Simon was going to be there. Jeff was a table-pounder—a short, heavy, little mess of a man with rumpled suit, pockmarked face and enough revolutionary zeal to equip a street full of anarchists. He was thirty-five, the oldest of the young group of lawyers who hung around together, and when the staff organized itself into a union a few years ago, Jeff was right out there on the barricades. Today he was union head in the criminal division. His fervor got a little boring, in fact it got boring as hell, but he was a nice guy and a good lawyer and he really worked like a bastard for the defendants. Also, he wasn't after Susan, and tonight that was about the biggest thing in his favor that I could think of.

"Hey, Peter," I said, "you haven't congratulated Susan yet." He was on a red leather ottoman wedged between a couple of end tables.

They all smiled brightly and turned expectantly to Susan.

"She just won her first case," I said.

"Oh, Susan," Helen said, "that's wonderful. You must be very proud."

"What was it?" Peter said, coughing again.

"Heckert," I said. "Richard Heckert. He hanged himself in his cell last night."

I laughed, and they all looked at me like I was some kind of ghoul. Everyone but Peter. He filled up his shot glass.

"I'm sorry, Susan," Helen said, and sat down on the other side of her.

Susan did not react. She'd never even met Heckert. The case was assigned to her two days ago because Heckert's original attorney retired. Even so, I was disappointed my little joke didn't get a rise out of her. She'd become some kind of accusation I had to keep putting down.

Helen was watching Susan closely. Helen was what you might call a little oversexed. She went for anything of the same species that hadn't died yet. I used to wonder if it was really cigarettes and whiskey that gave Peter that cough.

"Everybody's such a fucking coward," Jeff said. "When are they going to start telling the public what they really need?"

"So what do they need?" Susan said.

"Money, baby," Jeff said. "More judges, more DAs, more Legal Aid lawyers, more courtrooms—tons and tons and tons of money."

Now he had Susan's attention, and he decided to be the sage. "'How much money do you think you could raise if you could guarantee safety from mugging and burglary and rape for fifty dollars a person? Eight million people in New York? Could you get twenty million dollars? And if you asked for twenty million to provide a workable system of criminal justice, how much would you get?"

"Not one fuckin' dime," Peter shouted from the kitchen, and then walked in carefully, picking his steps, with a plate of crackers and cheese.

"I'd have done that, honey," Helen said.

Peter waved the bottle at her, like forget it, and emptied his shot glass.

"People are more interested in their own safety than they are in justice," Peter said, coughing. "So fuck 'em."

Susan got up to go into the bathroom and I sat down next to Helen.

"Don't you ever get tired of these heart-sucking little girls?" she asked. "They're so easy. No threats."

"Life has enough threats."

Susan came back and squeezed in between me and the

arm of the sofa. I put my arm around her. Everyone was silent for a minute.

"Well," Susan announced, as if delivering the conclusion to some complex philosophical theory she'd worked out on the john, "I'd sure hate like hell to do something wrong and end up in the Tombs or the Women's House of Detention."

"If you've done something wrong, you're okay," Peter said. "Just imagine being in there if you *haven't* done anything wrong. Guilt's the only ticket out. The last thing you want to be is innocent. It's much more important to conceal innocence than guilt. I had a client once who actually took the Fifth to keep from admitting he was innocent. The judge asked him a question, and he knew if he answered it truthfully the judge would know he was innocent and then wouldn't take his guilty plea. So he said, 'Your honor, I refuse to answer that question on the grounds that it might tend to disincriminate me.'"

I had to laugh. "Bullshit."

"Really. It really happened."

"And someday everything will happen," Jeff said. "Last winter they found out what a riot could do. They took hostages, they conned *The New York Times*, they got the Mayor to come in and listen to them. And now they tell the judges what kind of sentences they're willing to accept, how much time they'll accept. They've got the power."

"Jeffrey," Peter said, "they've got a helluva lot more power than they know. And when they find out—" He made an exploding gesture with his arms. Some bourbon sloshed out of the shot glass onto Susan's shirt. Jeff reached to wipe it off, but Helen beat him to it. She was there with a towel before Peter or Jeff or I could pull out a handkerchief.

I took Susan back to my apartment that night and we sat up very late talking. I lived in Tudor City, up high, with a view of the East River and a small private park. She spent half an hour walking up and down in front of book shelves examining titles. I showed her a common-place book I'd kept for years, thirty-seven pages of it nothing but definitions of justice. She asked me my favorite and I showed her one from Simone Weil. "Justice consists in seeing that no harm is done to men. Whenever a man cries inwardly, 'Why am I being hurt?' harm is being done to him. He is often mistaken when he tries to define the harm, and the why and by whom it is being inflicted upon him. But the cry itself is infallible."

"I guess you've heard that cry a lot," she said.

"So have you. You heard it from Alicia Bonner."

"Is that why Peter drinks so much?"

I laughed. "Maybe. I think he just likes the stuff. After what he's been through it's a wonder he's not in worse shape than he is."

"What do you mean?"

"He's been in the building too long, too many defendants. His brains have been strip-mined. Not to mention his soul."

"But you've been there longer than he has."

"I'm different. I'm a cynic. Remember?"

She was flipping through the quotes. "You must have been collecting these for years."

"I started in college. And in law school—in law school it got serious. I was terribly impressed by the nobility of

54

the law, and very proud of my association with it. I fed my vanity on all those gorgeous words. All that ethical horseshit."

She said nothing. The expression on her face—a thin but sympathetic smile—did not change. We sat down on a couch.

We were drinking Scotch, and every time she took a sip her tongue came forward to meet the edge of the glass and guide it back into her mouth. Her blue eyes blinked at me over the rim of the glass. It was hard to take. I was glad when she stood up again and started wandering around, looking things over. She stopped at a table with four chessboards on it.

"You play a lot of chess?"

"Not a lot."

"Four games at a time?"

"I play by mail, postcard chess."

"Doesn't that take a long time?"

"Yes."

"It's awfully impersonal."

"That's the best part."

The apartment looked nice with her walking around in it. In the seven years since I moved in, only two girls had actually lived there. One lasted seventeen months, the other two years. Both departed in the terminal stages of the I'm-getting-older-and-older-and-you'll-never-marry-me malady, the only treatment for which is the dishonest denial: "Oh, no, you're not," and, "Yes, maybe I will." I was too much of a coward for that.

I liked Susan there. I wanted her there. But I didn't want to fall in love with her. Life had enough threats.

The phone rang. I didn't move.

55

"Aren't you going to answer it?" she said.

"No."

"It might be important."

It kept ringing, five more rings. She said, "Really, don't you think you ought to answer it?"

"No. It doesn't bother me. I don't even hear it."

"But maybe it's important."

"Whenever my phone rings," I said, "I think if there's anyone in the world at that moment I'd like to talk to. Then I think if there's any possibility that it's that person calling. If there's not, then I don't answer the phone. It's a trick I learned from my father. He could sit in a room for hours with a ringing phone."

"You're weird."

"People are much too quick to answer telephones."

"Your watch only has one hand."

"You noticed."

"I noticed a long time ago. You're very strange."

"I don't think that's strange. I dropped my watch on the floor and it was upside down with the crystal off, and when I picked it up the minute hand caught on a piece of fiber from the carpet and broke off. So I put the crystal back on and planned to get the hand fixed. Then I discovered I could tell time very well by the hour hand alone. Time is one-dimensional. It doesn't need two indicators. A sundial only has one hand. I can tell time as accurately without the minute hand as I could before with it. So why have it fixed? Why have the minute hand put back when it's superfluous?"

She shrugged. I hadn't convinced her.

"Why is that strange?" I said.

56

"I don't know. Don't make a big thing out of it. You just see a man with a watch that only has one hand, and then you find out he's got a whole routine about not answering his phone, and you begin to think he's a little weird."

She was smiling. I had the feeling that the weirder I was the better she'd like it.

"Have you ever been married?" she asked.

"Once."

"What happened?"

"She left me."

"Did you love her?"

"Very much."

She looked dubious.

"Does that surprise you?" I said.

"No. Of course not. But I thought . . ."

"What? Go ahead. Say it."

"I thought you were probably one of those honeymoon types. Very good on honeymoons but can't handle a whole marriage. They seduce, but they don't love. It wouldn't even occur to them to fall in love if they'd never heard about it."

We sat there together, just sipping the Scotch and not saying anything. I thought about starting something, but I didn't. Careful with this one.

"I'm sorry I seem like so much of a cynic to you," I said, meaning it. I was getting a little drunk.

She didn't say anything.

"You know, when you get into your middle forties, you find out the falseness of a lot of your old ideals. Things you would have died for turn out to be myths. You realize you've been betrayed, you've betrayed yourself. All you're left with is reality."

"That's heavy."

Yeah, that's heavy. A real downer. Why do they talk like that?

It was three o'clock and she said she had to go. I took her home in a taxi and asked her up to my farm for a weekend. She said she'd think about it.

■

I had a wife once, a gorgeous narcissist from Minerva, Ohio. Her father owned a snowplow factory. She went to Wellesley. Rich, bright, mixed up. We lived in a $300,000 converted stable in Washington Mews. We lived there fifteen years, and had a son. Then she started going mad. She had long blond hair and began wearing it down the front of her face, with just a tiny separation she could peek through. She never went out. She sat around with her head in her hands and the hair hiding her face. And then she stopped getting out of bed, stopped even waking up. That was in late 1965. New York was starting to go to hell then. We had always loved it together. And then it started coming unglued, it wasn't fun anymore, it was turning into a terrible place to live. And my wife was going insane. I watched New York and my wife go mad together. She went to Payne Whitney for a month and then came home. Two days later she was sick again. She went in and out of Payne Whitney five times in fourteen months. Then one day I came back from court and she was gone. I couldn't believe it. For two years I hadn't even been able to get her out of bed. She was terrified of everything outside the house, outside her bedroom, outside her bed.

It took four days to trace her ticket through the American Express charge. She'd gone to San Francisco. Her doctor said, "That sometimes happens, a desperate lunge for safety. It may be best. Often the mind knows what's best."

Except that I loved her.

My son was seventeen. He stayed around for six months and then took off for Europe. He thought he was Ernest Hemingway. He liked to fight and write. He fought in the streets and won, in school and won, and in the Golden Gloves, where a six-foot-three-inch black sixteen-year-old demolished him. He went to Paris. He thought he'd be part of the new lost generation, a bunch of hippies hanging around the Latin Quarter. He fled into the past. And my wife into the future. No one wants the present. They both ran in opposite directions. Not from each other— from me, from New York. Two pieces of late '60s American shrapnel. And me, ice-o-lated.

FOUR

I WAS GETTING SCARED. The Alicia Bonner experience hadn't worn off. Of course, it wasn't just Alicia Bonner. It was all the others before her—the suicides, murders, rapes. All the madmen. It was too much. It was breaking through. The protective restraints were cracking.

Seventeen years ago when I first started this job I made the mistake of talking to the complainant, the victim, in a rape and robbery case. She was a pretty little blonde in her twenties. A Negro teen-ager jumped her in the park. She stood there in court with a crowd around and tears streaming down her cheeks and told me what my client had done to her, and how vile she thought I was for defending him. She went hysterical. It was like the Koran yelling at me, "He who defends the guilty accuses the just." I gave the case to someone else in the office. After that I made it a point never to look at the complainants. If I had anything to do with them, I couldn't practice. Well, now it had gone a step further. I'd become too emotional about the defendants, my clients.

I was having strange and dangerous thoughts. I believed our judicial system was one of the most exquisite creations of man. But then I began to see that the structure built to manifest that system—the police, courts, jails —was sick and crumbling. I saw that I wasn't really working within the system. I was working within the structure. The system said how things should be. The structure was how they were. I saw that the structure was no longer adequately representing the system. If I were going to be loyal to the system, I would have to forsake what was left of this collapsing structure. I would have to destroy it.

I badly needed to talk to someone and find out if they agreed with me or if they thought I was crazy. Sonigo would only cough and laugh. Fischer was on the other team. I knew only one man, intelligent and feeling, who understood the system—and the structure—and had fully accommodated himself to it emotionally and intellectually. Judge Joe Bianchi.

I asked him to have dinner with me. He suggested a night the next week when I had promised to talk about plea bargaining at a symposium he ran for New York University law students. I wanted to do it sooner than that and he agreed to meet me that evening.

He was working late in his chambers so we went to a restaurant near the court building. I told him I had this idea that I wasn't working for the system anymore but for this decaying, wretched structure, that I was betraying the system.

He agreed with me. "But it's the only structure there is, Al. I've thought about it for years. What can you do? Right now there really isn't anything you can do."

I shook my head, and was sorry I had called him.

"Well, what *can* you do?" he said. "Ask for an appointment with the PJs? Rhein won't listen to you, and if he did he wouldn't do anything. Remember, Al, I know

Rhein. I know Halley. I know Rubinstein. I know them all. I've had them on my back for years. You can imagine. Rhein's got a heart like a hockey puck—hard, tough, and black."

"And cold," I said. Rhein was Presiding Justice of the Appellate Division's First Department, covering Manhattan and the Bronx. In effect that made him Bianchi's boss and gave him enormous power over damned near everyone else too. I had a sign in the window of my apartment over the fire escape. "The apartment you are about to burglarize is occupied by Justice S. P. Rhein, Appellate Division, New York State Supreme Court." I hadn't had any trouble in seven years.

A big part of Rhein's responsibility was court reform, so if you were looking for someone to blame and hate, he made a good and worthy target.

"Yeah," Bianchi said. "And cold. I forgot cold. You know what he says when you try to tell him how bad things are? He holds up his hand and he says, 'Wait. Let me tell *you* how bad things are.' And then he quotes numbers at you. I get memos and reports every day, Al. You don't see it. You want to hear some numbers? Our backlog of criminal cases is seven hundred thousand. Seven. Hundred. Thousand. If no new arrests were made, Al, none at all, if the whole police department went on vacation, you know how long it would take to dispose of just that backlog? Two and a half years, Al. We're getting more than six thousand indictments a year, and we're capable of trying maybe a hundred and fifty."

I'd heard these statistics before. I started to say something to turn him off.

"No, Al, no. Listen to me. A man commits a felony, his

chances of not even being arrested are better than four to one. If he *is* arrested, his chances of getting indicted are only one in five. If he *is* indicted, the chances of the charge being reduced before trial are ten to one. See how hard it is to get into jail? That's a *very* exclusive place, jail is. To get there you got to be one of the dumbest, poorest, unluckiest guys alive. Or else you got to work at it so long eventually the odds catch up with you. Of all the defendants waiting court appearances, you know how many are in jail? Two percent, Al. The other ninety-eight percent are out on bail or parole, robbing and stealing. The planned capacity of the Tombs is nine hundred and thirty-two. Actual population as of yesterday was two thousand one hundred and eleven. That means some of those nine-by-six-foot cells have three men in them, the third guy sleeping on the floor. And people ask if we're gonna have more riots. They put you on the floor of a nine-by-six-foot cell run over by mice with two other men in it, would you riot, Al? Fucking yes you'd riot. Last time, even the guards were on the side of the inmates. The papers had that. I'll tell you something between us the papers didn't have. Certain of those guards are saying that in the next riot, they're rioting *with* the inmates. So you can't tell the PJs about how bad it is, Al. They can tell you maybe."

I didn't want to listen to any more.

"So what are you gonna do?" he said. "After the hundreds of studies and reports, what're you gonna do? These people don't need to be informed, Al, they need to be *moved*. And how are you gonna do that? For that you'd need a gun. You're gonna kidnap their children or something? And don't quote me on that. Some people, they heard I said that, they might not be so sure I was kidding."

When I was a child I used to wonder what, if anything, might be accepted as justification for violating the admonition posted above fare boxes on Fifth Avenue buses. Might one be pardoned a brief, frantic word to the driver in the case of a heart attack, childbirth, armed robbery? I saw those words everywhere, and heard them. At home. At school. Wherever authority was made to tolerate intrusion. "We wrote the book, we know what we're doing, so just shut up and don't talk to the driver."

And now I had heard them, or something very like them, from Bianchi.

I went home. The whole evening had depressed the hell out of me.

That Friday I got out the Porsche and drove to the country with Susan. I've got eighty acres in upstate New York, a pear-shaped piece of woods and meadows with just the tip of the pear touching the road, so when you drive in and get to the house, in the center of the pear, you can't see anything anywhere except my property. There's no chance of any of the developers around there putting roads past my house or trailer camps next door or frozen custard stands or anything. I get out there every weekend, with the tulips and the vegetables and this old mare called Molly, and I start to feel human again. I almost begin to forget about court and the detention pens and the Tombs and all those defendants, and complainants and witnesses and . . .

The house is two stories, and across my road from it,

next to a large pasture, there's an old barn I don't use. Up the road further there's a chicken house, really falling down, and near the house, maybe thirty yards, there's a garage.

I took Susan inside the house and apologized for the furniture, which was practically nonexistent, just beds and a TV and one sofa and a lot of rugs and cushions around. I went out in the woods and collected some wood and built a fire in a brick barbecue between the house and the garage. We'd brought a huge striped bass and we stuffed it with fennel and butter and grilled it over the wood fire. I laid a blanket next to the fire and we sat there in the glow and ate the fish and drank white wine iced in a bucket. All you could hear was the fire and woods noises and wind in the trees. We stared into the fire, and ate and talked, and then lay back and looked up at the stars. Manhattan was a billion miles away.

"What are you thinking about?" I said.

"Nothing."

So we both just lay there. I thought about the stars, and then about Susan, and then my mind started coming back to court and to this problem of mine. I'd make a conscious effort to stop thinking about it, and think about Susan and how nice it was here, how good the bass had been, but the problem always came back. I saw Alicia Bonner, and then I remembered lots of other cases, defendants I'd forgotten about and not thought of for months or years. This kid who got a walk and wanted to borrow five hundred dollars from me to go in on a grocery store, so I gave it to him, never thinking to get it back. Then five months later he came in with a fistful of twenties and paid me off, and a week after that I had him as a client again, locked up for armed robbery, which of course is where he got the twenties.

"What are you thinking about?" Susan said.

We were lying on our backs and she came up on one elbow and looked down at me. Her hair reflected the color of the fire.

"Nothing."

"You were thinking about court."

"How did you know?"

"I could feel it. I was thinking the same thing when you asked me, but I didn't want to remind you of it."

I put my hand on her hair and moved her face down and kissed her. Now was the time for the moonlight and roses, the flattery, the smile, the gentle touch. But I decided to be honest, which has its points too. She was a serious girl, more serious than she looked, and she admired the selfless devotion of this brilliant, rich attorney who gave his career to rescuing the downtrodden. So I said what I had really been thinking.

"You know, I feel like I've been standing over a crack in the earth, one foot in the world of this farm, a nice world of grilled bass and Chablis and a wonderful girl, a nice apartment, television, the theater, restaurants. And the other foot is in the world of jails and psychosis and poverty and murder, robbery, suicide. And the crack keeps getting wider and wider and wider. Pretty soon if I don't lift one foot or the other I'm gonna be split right up the crotch."

"I'd say you've got a problem." She was looking down at me, smiling, trying to be playful and not let me get as solemn as it looked like I was going to get.

"I'm giving a little talk Friday night to an NYU class

Bianchi has, on plea bargaining. By then I'm going to have an answer."

"An answer?" She sat up and crossed her legs, pulling her ankles in under her.

"I've decided I'm going to do something. I'm not going to keep on with this bullshit. It's immoral. You know the poem by E. E. Cummings about a conscientious objector? There's a line in it: 'There is some shit I will not eat.' That's where I am. Someday this stopgap plea-bargaining charade is going to fail, and then the whole structure will collapse. It'll be like a disease that's finally acquired immunity to the antibiotics and spreads faster and stronger than ever. The whole structure's dying, Susan. You can hear the screams. I don't want to stand there and watch everybody suffering while it dies. I'd rather kill it than do that."

"Judicial euthanasia," she said, still playful.

"Right."

"Al, I don't understand."

"I don't either. I'm just talking. I don't know what to do."

"How could you kill it?"

"I don't know. I'm just trying to think. If a town needs a new school and everyone is arguing about do they really need a new school, maybe the old one is okay for a few more years, maybe another coat of paint is all it needs, everybody's procrastinating and thinking about it and no one wants to take the responsibility and say, 'Okay, damn it, get up the money, we're gonna build a new fuckin' *school*,' what can you do? You can go out to the school some night and just set the thing on fire and burn it down. And then no one has to make a decision anymore, do they need a new school or not. All they have to decide is do they want a school at all. Period. You make it easy for them."

"Is that what you're going to do?"

"I don't know."

"How could you do it? You can't burn down the criminal court building."

"I'm not sure."

"But you've got an idea."

"No, I don't."

That was a lie. I did have an idea. But I knew if I told her we'd be talking about it all night, and that wasn't what I wanted to do all night.

"Let's go inside," I said. "The fire's going out."

We had Armagnac on the couch in the living room, and then I showed her the roof. The house is on a hill and the people who had the farm before me put turf up on the roof, which is almost flat, and planted some kind of grass and ground cover up there, and on clear nights it's a nice place to take a drink, smell the air, feel the breeze and look out over the lights of the county. And you get there through my bedroom.

Tonight there was no seduction. No grasp and fumble. No coy protests. She just decided very simply that she wanted to make love. An honest girl, very enlightened, a product of the modern permissiveness one hears so viciously maligned.

In the middle of the night she woke up and said the scraping of a branch on the window had scared her. I told her there weren't any branches by the window, it must have been the mice.

"You have mice?"

"All these old country houses have mice."

"Why don't you get rid of them?"

"They're not hurting anything. They don't know they're not supposed to be here. Maybe they are supposed to be here. They're happy to coexist. Why shouldn't I be?"

"Wow. Ask him the time, he tells you how to build a watch. It was just a simple question."

We lay there quietly for a while, and then she started talking again. She told me about her family, about her grandfather who'd owned a bar in Lodi, New Jersey, and her father who managed a Holiday Inn, and her brother who was a civil engineer with the Port Authority, and why she became a lawyer, which was because she wanted to do something for people and she didn't want to be a teacher or a doctor.

I asked her—it was unfeeling of me, I know, but we were in the dark—if it was true that she had watched her brother fire a shot at her father. She said it was not true. "He watched me. I fired the shot. It was my brother's gun, but I fired it. I hated my father. I didn't think that much of my mother either. They were both a couple of vicious bastards."

I was amazed. She said it so matter-of-factly. No emotion at all. I thought about that for a while, lying there in the dark, making too much of it maybe—was I naïve, or was she so tough, or did I just not understand her at all? Then she said something about liking the low bed because she could reach her arm out and rest it on the rug as if she were at the beach lying on a blanket in the sun. Then we went back to sleep and didn't get out of bed until noon. She fixed breakfast and I took her for a walk in the woods, along a stream filled with trout. She asked me if I ever fished for the trout. I said, "No, they're my friends." She agreed that it would not be nice to fish for one's friends.

I wondered if she meant it. Or if someplace deep inside she was thinking that between the mice and the trout I had an excessively sentimental regard for the welfare of dumb animals.

■

My attorney just left. He is not optimistic. One way or another, he thinks they will finish me.

"They will do what they have to do," he says. "We can go through all the motions, but in the end they will do what they have to do."

"Well, let's go through the motions anyway," I said. "I am very interested in going through all the motions."

"Of course," he said. "I just want you to know the realities. I don't want to mislead you."

We talked for half an hour and he left.

Perhaps the confinement is affecting me. I am having trouble keeping truth straight. I spend a lot of time pacing the cell, straightening out my mind. Memories and convictions crumble and spill. I shore up partitions, patch holes, put everything back where it belongs. But I am learning that truth and lie are no more distinct from each other than time and space. The basic problem: how to know the right thing and do it, how to fail minimally.

FIVE

HERE WAS my idea. Not mine, really—it had been around for years. I'd heard it mentioned a number of times, but I don't think anyone before had ever seriously set out to put it into action.

It was simple: If none of the defendants agreed to plead guilty, the criminal justice structure would be destroyed within a month. Every day some four hundred felons from city jails pleaded guilty in court and were either released or transferred to upstate prisons. That was Supreme Court, where felonies were handled. It didn't count defendants processed on minor charges in Criminal Court. Now if none of these Supreme Court defendants, who made up the bulk of the jail population, agreed to plead guilty, then the jail population would increase by four hundred inmates a day. The total backlog of felony cases in the courts would similarly increase. The structure, unable to contain that increase, would hemorrhage and collapse. It would no longer be possible to study or consider in what way the present structure might be improved. If any criminal justice structure was to be had at all, it would be necessary to build a new one from scratch.

I thought the plan would work, but I was not at all

sure I should try it. There were a lot of problems, not the least of them confidence and courage. I was certain the structure was causing great suffering and that it ought to be destroyed. But was I certain enough to see the belief converted into blood? What is the morally acceptable price of justice when the currency is blood?

I carried these questions around with me for a week, the week after my weekend in the country with Susan. That Tuesday I almost had the will. I was looking through the bars of the detention pen, talking to a young black in jeans and a T-shirt who'd been in six months for a daytime burglary. I'd got him an offer of time served, but it was his first arrest and he didn't know what to do. He'd spent the whole six months telling everyone who'd listen—his mother, his father, his brothers, sisters, friends, everyone he knew in jail—telling everyone that he didn't do it, that he just looked like the guy who did it, that it was mistaken identification. He couldn't bring himself to get up in court and admit he'd done it.

I told him the offer, and he just plain didn't know what to do. He said, "Man, they just bribin' me to say I did it."

I told him I'd never heard it put any better, but that he had to admit it was a very attractive bribe.

Then another man in the pen, an old-timer with a huge Afro with a white comb sticking out of it, said to the kid, "Man, don't you take no plea. Can't you see what he's doin'? Them Legal Aids' all the same as the DA, man. They workin' for the DA tryin' t'get everyone to say they guilty. They worse than the DA, man, 'cause they sup- posed to be helpin' you, be on your side. Don' listen to him, man. Make 'em give you a trial. You en*tit*led to a

78

trial, man. Don' take no plea. I ain't gonna take no plea. I'm innocent, man. I'm goin' to trial. They gonna have to *prove* I ain't innocent."

All through this speech, which, believe me, I have heard many times before, I was thinking, "Okay, Dori, here's your chance. Now might you do it pat."

The kid looked at me to see what I thought of this advice he was getting. I wouldn't even have had to speak. I could have done it with a look. Just a nod of agreement, and he would have refused the offer.

I told him to remember that if he took the plea he'd walk, and then he could tell his family and friends anything he wanted. He'd be out. I told him to think about that for a while, and then he'd be called upstairs.

And when they called him up, he copped out.

I was suspicious of my motives.

Maybe it wasn't compassion and an interest in justice that was urging me to do this. Maybe it was ego.

On the other hand, I thought of Oliver Wendell Holmes: "What have we better than a blind guess to show that the criminal law in its present form does more good than harm?"

What was wrong with opposing an unjust structure? Again, Holmes: "Law is the business to which my life is devoted, and I should show less than devotion if I did not do what in me lies to improve it."

Not to act, not to *resist*, would be immoral. I might have some excuse for inaction if the structure were providing justice to anyone—to defendants, or complainants, or witnesses, or the community. To *anyone*. But it was not.

Finally I knew what had to be done. Justice should be

the strongest element in any society. Any judicial structure weak enough to be destroyed by one man, should be. I decided to move.

I knew that once I started telling clients not to plead guilty, I could count on the help of other Legal Aid lawyers, probably a number of Assistant DAs, and even some judges. But the Tombs inmates themselves could give more assistance than anyone. I wanted the help of someone who could influence them, someone who could explain to them how powerful they really were and, most important, how they could use that power. For more than a year, there'd been a group called Prisoners' Lib with members in and out of the city jails. They read newspapers, they read books, they knew their rights. They had even organized a march on the Tombs that had caused a few anxious moments when officers inside feared it might touch off a riot.

So Thursday morning I called the Tombs and said I wanted an interview that afternoon with a client named Oscar Butterfield.

Butterfield was, simply, the meanest man alive. And sinister. Sinister is meanness plus brains, and a psychological report on Oscar said he had an IQ of 158. He was black, about six five, 270 pounds, completely bald, bearded. His head looked as if all the hair falling from his scalp had grabbed hold of his chin and grown desperately long and heavy just to apologize. A pencil-thick welt scarred his right cheek from mouth to earlobe. He chewed hard candy. He had a way of listening quietly to a man, sucking gently on an inch-thick ball of butterscotch nestled back behind some giant molar. Then suddenly, explosively, his tongue reached back there and fired the candy across his mouth, sent it crashing from tooth to tooth, banging back and forth like a runaway pinball. The effect often left those around him too rattled to get on with business.

When I got to the Tombs, Oscar was already in the counsel room, waiting on a bench with other inmates. The room contained fourteen small cubicles, each with a table and two chairs. Oscar rose from the bench, and we walked to an empty cubicle. He wedged himself through the narrow door and sat down, his long thick legs twining around the furniture.

He had pleaded guilty to two heroin sales in exchange for a sentence of 0–3 years, the precise amount to be determined after a probation report. With his record that meant something very close to the maximum three. Now, chewing candy, he said he wanted to withdraw his plea. He had no idea why he had been called down to see me, but he was taking advantage of the meeting.

"There's guys upstairs got a lot less than me for two sales," he said, sucking on the candy. "I shouldn't get no more than three months on each."

"Look, Oscar," I said, "please don't fence with me. You're no kid. You've been in and out. You know damned well you face a possible seven years on each of these."

I didn't want to have to go through all this. I was anxious to get on to my own business.

He pretended sullenness. "I don't care. I don't care about no seven years each if I blow it. I'm goin' to bat. And I don't want no lawyer. I'm goin' to bat all by myself."

"You have a perfect right to do that," I said.

He grinned. I knew Oscar, and I knew he was playing. I also knew there would be nothing serious with him unless I let him finish his act.

"How much can I get?" he asked.

"Seven on each. Fourteen all together."

"Can't you get me probation?"

"You know I can't."

"Time served?"

"Oscar, you know I can't."

"One and one running wild?" That's two one-year sentences served consecutively.

"Oscar, that's impossible with your record."

Now he gave me the indignant act. I'd insulted him. "What's *wrong* with my record? I ain't never done *nothin'!*"

"I've seen your record, Oscar. It's almost four sheets. You know that."

"I ain't never tortured no one. I ain't no mad-dog murderer. What's wrong with my record? I ain't never done nothin'."

He banged the candy around for a while and then gave me a wide smile. "So I stay with the zip to three. What do I tell the probation officer when he comes to see me?"

"Tell him everything good about yourself."

"That don't give me much to say."

"Pull at his heartstrings. Give him some candy."

He laughed. "Yeah, man." He stood up, ready to leave. He raised a fist. "Right on."

"Don't leave yet," I said. "You don't even know why I wanted to see you."

He sat down quickly, happy for the reprieve. He'd have stayed there all day.

"I've got sort of a proposition for you, Oscar. Something that might work out better than that zip to three."

"Yeah?" No smile now. No tough look. Just sucking on the candy. Ready.

"Oscar, what do you think would happen if none of the defendants took guilty pleas, if they all stopped pleading guilty?"

He stared at me blankly, thinking. I said nothing and waited.

"Things'd get might crowded up there."

I kept waiting.

"I guess sooner or later . . ." He stopped. All the alternatives were too outrageous to suggest. He was afraid of sounding foolish. "You tell me," he said finally.

"You had it yourself, Oscar. The whole thing would explode. The system couldn't work. One way or another it'd all blow up."

He did not move. He kept staring at me deadpan and sucking on the candy.

"Some people on the outside, Oscar, myself included, think the whole structure needs rebuilding. And before it can be rebuilt it has to be torn down. We think the fastest way to tear it down is to stop all these guilty pleas. All I'd like you to do, Oscar, is think about that. And maybe talk about it with some of the other inmates. Not the idiots and lunatics. The ones who know what's going on. Talk about it. Think about it. That's all."

He nodded quickly several times and sat quietly. Then he said, "Yeah, man. I'll do that."

"Thanks."

I walked out of the Tombs feeling as if I'd left a bomb behind.

83

The next night, Friday night, I had my scheduled dinner with Bianchi. Although by that time I was convinced of what I would do, I said nothing to him. After dinner we walked across Washington Square Park to NYU. The meeting with the students was in a modern, rich-looking chrome-and-leather conference room. Bianchi introduced me to the students as they arrived. There were about twenty of them, almost all men, dressed in jeans, long hair. I said I'd like to make a few general remarks about the plea-bargaining process, and after that they could ask questions. Just in case any of them might not know, I explained what plea bargaining was, roughly how it worked, and then said, "Now, where is plea bargaining taking us? If it continues to flourish and grow until every case results in a guilty plea—and we are very nearly at that point now—then arrest will equal guilt automatically. There will be no recognition of innocence, and we will be without justice. And without a great many other things besides.

"But there is another possible path. If the opposite occurs, and the plea-bargaining trend is abruptly reversed, and there are *no* guilty pleas, then the pressure within the entire structure will increase very rapidly and we will have an explosion."

They were listening. Talk of violence always interests the young.

Bianchi looked worried.

"Which of these two possibilities is the more desirable, or the least undesirable? The first has the advantage of leaving us with the appearance of some kind of judicial apparatus—police, jails, courts. But there is no justice, and very little order. The system has been suppressed and neutralized.

"The second possibility is more violent. It has the advantage, however, of destroying only the structure of justice—the police, jails, and courts—and leaves the underlying system itself intact. The absence of justice is visible —horribly, violently visible—and therefore the need for repair is obvious and would no doubt be answered.

"You may decide for yourselves which is the better alternative. Let me just add that one enormous advantage of the first is that it requires nothing from you, or me, or Judge Bianchi, or anyone else. Nothing but inaction. That can be a comfort."

One or two of them smiled at that and glanced at Bianchi.

He was not smiling.

One of the girls, a pretty blonde with an extraordinary chest, said, "Mr. Dori, you list these two alternatives, neither of them very attractive, and seem to say they're a natural, an inevitable outgrowth of plea bargaining. Why is it so inevitable? Isn't there some other possibility?"

"I would love to think so, but I don't see any. I think we got into plea bargaining in the first place because of an unwillingness to take the steps—very expensive steps— that were necessary to adapt to changing conditions. When things stopped working well and we had to make compromises, the first compromise we made was the least expensive financially—we compromised individual justice. I don't mean justice only for the accused. I mean for everyone. Paying very strict, fastidious attention to *individual* justice is terribly, terribly expensive. It takes lots of peo-

85

ple—police, judges, lawyers, probation officers, doctors, guards—lots of courts, jails, police stations. So we slacked off. We saved money. But when justice for the individual erodes, the strength and safety of society erode. As you lose individual justice, you lose group justice. Then you lose the appearance of justice, then the belief in justice. Individual justice has already disappeared, and now you are about to see society collapse. You are. You will see."

There were some shaking heads, some sighs, some nervous smiles. Bianchi took advantage of the pause to stand up and thank me for coming and put an end to it all. After the last student had left he said, "Come on, Dori, we're gonna have a drink before you get yourself killed."

We walked through the park to a bar on University Place. All the way Bianchi didn't say a word. He was thinking and saving it up for when we got to the bar. I was bracing myself, telling myself not to let him bully me. He was a strong man, aggressive, persuasive. I'd seen him go to work on some very heavy attorneys and leave them quiet and subdued as puppies. I was going to hold my own and tell him what I thought and what I was going to do, and I wanted to make him agree with me. I wanted his approval.

We walked through a crowd of students at the bar and took a back table and ordered Scotch. When the waitress left, Bianchi gave me his stern-but-kind grandfatherly look and said, "Al, we've known each other a long time. We've worked together a long time. And we've trusted each other a long time. We've taken some risks together and I don't think either of us has ever lost any sleep worrying about the other's loyalty. So I'm asking you quietly, calmly, simply. Have you gone out of your fucking *mind*?"

"Not at all. I think that maybe what I've done is come into my fucking mind."

"Then just exactly what did you mean, 'If the trend is reversed and there are no guilty pleas'?"

"Just that. The only people who've been giving the structure a helping hand are the defendants. They've got the guilty pleas the government needs, and they're selling them for time. If they stop selling them, then the pressure builds up and the structure explodes."

"And you intend to encourage that?"

"I intend to *do* it."

"You *have* lost your mind."

He took a sip of his drink. "You told those students they were about to see society collapse."

"You think it won't?"

"If you do what you're thinking about, maybe it will. Do you want that?"

"Don't you? Think about it. Try to put emotion aside and just think about it objectively. What's so great about society? I mean superficially, right now. Are you delighted with it? Do you enjoy inhaling poison gas? Do you like walking through filthy streets? Do you feel safe and comfortable on the subway? Does your garbage always get picked up? How many times has your house been burglarized? Do you enjoy deafening noise? Has your wife been raped yet? Do you worry about getting mugged?"

"That's not society."

"Then what is it? This city has become a toilet, Joe. It's time to flush. Pull the chain."

He took another drink, slowly. "There'll be a lot of blood running down that drain," he said.

"Maybe some of it'll be mine."

He looked up sharply. "I don't think you really believe that. But you're right. Let's talk about that. There are a lot of people who wouldn't stand around and let you get away with something like that. Some of them are pretty rough people. I've been up against them once or twice myself, Al. They have a lot to protect. Never under-estimate the ruthlessness of a man protecting the status quo. You could get hurt very badly."

"I know."

"I'm not talking about your career."

"I'm not naïve, Joe."

More drinking. More silence.

"Maybe you're just spiteful," Bianchi said. "Maybe you want to destroy something because you think it's been destroying you. Maybe you don't like the authority."

"I don't like authority that's phony and bogus, that doesn't let people be heard, that doesn't give a shit for people. No one gets heard anymore. Well, I'm going to shout very, very loudly, and when I'm through I'll be heard."

"Okay, Al. But do one thing. Promise me one thing."

"What?"

"Ask yourself this, and think about it. Take a few min-utes every day and think about it. Are you *sure* you know why you're doing it? Answer that question to yourself, and keep answering it."

"I have answered it," I said, "and I'll keep on answering it. Every day."

"And beware the lust for justice, Al. Justice has killed more people than it's saved."

"That can't be known."

Monday morning Bianchi came quickly into court, sat

down and didn't even look at me. My first case was a short, thin, very pale young white man with a goatee and thick welts across the insides of his forearms. I knew they were suicide slashes, but asked him anyway.

"I do things I don't know about sometimes," he said.

He'd been arrested with a loaded gun in a West Side bar. I told him I hadn't talked to the judge yet. "What're you looking for?"

"I'm lookin' to get outa here."

"Well, they're not gonna give you a walk."

He had a three-page sheet and had only been in ten months.

"I'll take a bullet."

A bullet for him, with his ten months in and two off for good behavior, would have been a walk. And there was no way in the world he'd get less than two years. He was a habitual A&R man who was very obviously going to go right out and stick up another bar. I'd have advised him to take two years if he had the chance. But not today. I said, "So you want a bullet, and if you don't get a bullet I take it you want a trial?"

"Yeah."

"Fine."

In court, Fischer looked at the sheet and said to Bianchi, "I'll say one thing for him, your honor. He's a hard worker. He's really dedicated to his trade."

"I'll give him a D with a top of five," Bianchi said, glancing through the grand jury extract. "Not that he deserves it. He deserves twenty years."

"I just spoke to him, your honor," I said. "He wants a bullet."

Fischer laughed.

"He says if he can't have a bullet he'll go to trial."

"The guy's bananas," Fischer said.

"A most perceptive diagnosis, David, and you haven't even seen the patient."

"Okay," Bianchi said. "You want to mark that ready for trial, Dave?" And then to the clerk. "Call the next case, please."

The next was a huge black woman the shape and color of a cannonball. She had on an orange miniskirt and sneakers with white socks. She had a long record of robbing old people in subways. She knew her way around, or thought she did.

Her last subway job had left an old man with a broken hip. The offer was two years. She wanted time served, which was thirteen months.

"Your honor," Fischer said with pain on his face, "that guy was eighty-four years old. The doctor says he'll never walk again. She's got a three-page sheet. Two years is a ridiculously low offer."

Bianchi looked at me. "He's right, Al. You know he's right. She ought to snap at two years. Next time around she probably won't get it again."

"I'm definitely not putting it down as an offer," Fischer said. "If she doesn't take it now it'll never be repeated."

I talked to her again. "You want time served, right?"

"Yeah, man. I didn't kill nobody. I know somebody got two years for a homicide. I don't deserve no two years on this here."

"So you don't want the two years?"

"No, man."

I went back to the bench. "Sorry. She says she has

friends who kill people for two years. An offer of two years on this offends her sense of justice."

Fischer looked at me strangely and then looked at Bianchi. Bianchi said, "Next case."

They brought up a young man, a Vietnam veteran with a Distinguished Service Cross. He'd grabbed a woman's purse on Central Park West, then emptied a .45 automatic at pursuing police. He missed them.

"An E with a top of three," Bianchi said.

Fischer read through his file and nodded. "Okay."

I went out in the hall by the pen stairs and they walked him up. He was furious. "What the fuck is this? I been locked up fourteen months, and I ain't done nothin'. All I done is grab some lady's handbag. Okay, I done that. But that don't mean they got a right to lock me up no fourteen months."

"You also emptied a gun at the cops," I said.

"That's what *they* say, man. Tell me if I emptied a gun at them cops why I didn't hit none of 'em. Tell me that."

"Well, it's not what I think that counts. They're offering a Class E felony with a maximum of three years."

"*Three years!* For stealin' a purse? Man, I ain't gonna take no shit like that."

"You don't want it?"

"Hell no, I don't want it."

"He doesn't want it," I said to Bianchi and Fischer. "He says three years is an excessive sentence for purse snatching."

Fischer was disgusted. "Did he say anything about the attempted murder of three police officers?"

I knew Bianchi couldn't go below three years on this,

so I thought I'd at least run through the motions of trying to work out a plea. "No one was injured, your honor."

"Your honor," Fischer said, "he shouldn't get credit for being a poor shot."

"Well," I said, "it's certainly important to the men he shot at that he's a poor shot."

"This could have been a triple homicide, your honor. It's not his fault it wasn't a triple homicide. If the Army taught their men how to shoot better, it would—"

"All right," Bianchi said. "I can't give him anything less than a top of three on this, Al."

"He won't take it."

Bianchi sighed, made a note on his calendar and said, "Next case."

The next two cases had private lawyers so I took a seat in the jury box. While they waited for one of the lawyers to talk things over with his client, Fischer sat down next to me.

"You don't seem to be having much luck today," he said.

"Well if the DA would stop encouraging the infliction of such unjustly harsh sentences on all my clients . . ."

"Yeah, it's terrible. But I kind of get the impression you're not trying too hard today."

He was gazing out into the spectators.

I didn't answer.

Just before lunch we got the kind of case I hadn't been looking forward to, one that had to expose clearly what I was up to. A Puerto Rican named Jose Alvarez was offered a year for a single sale of heroin. I did not encourage him to accept it, and he did not.

At the bench I said, "No go."

Fischer gave me a very strong, inquiring, suspicious look.

"*No go!*" he said. "What do you mean, 'No go'?"

He looked at Alvarez's sheet, a long one. "He knows the price. He knows it's a year for a single sale. That's so solid they practically post it in the station houses. One sale costs one year."

"He says he's not buying."

"He thinks the price is gonna go down? Man, if that offer goes anywhere, it'll be up. Doesn't he know we're in an inflationary economy?"

"I can't tell him how to plead, Dave. If he thinks a year is too high, he's got every right to deny it and demand a trial. Maybe he's innocent."

"Maybe I don't shit every morning."

Fischer looked at Bianchi, expecting help from him. Bianchi seemed tired. He stared at me for a minute, and we talked with our eyes. "You sure, Al?"

"I'm sure."

Fischer studied me, then turned and looked at Bianchi, then back at me. "Hey, what's going on here? What's happening? Is there something I should know about?"

Bianchi recessed for lunch. Fischer followed me out of court.

"What the hell's happening, Al?"

We were getting into a crowded elevator and I didn't want to talk. Fischer walked with me out to the street.

"Are you busy for lunch?" I said.

We went to Carlo's and sat in a booth.

"What's going on, Dave, is this. What do you think would happen if none of the defendants pleaded guilty?"

Fischer looked at me for a moment, thinking. Then he grinned. "You bastard," he said. Then he laughed. "Man, you are a fucking *bastard.*"

"Exactly," I said.

"You'll never get away with it."

"Why?"

"Because they'll run your ass right out of court. As soon as Rhein gets a look at the calendar report from Part Seven he'll see what's happening and he'll call Billings and you'll be out of court on your ass." Billings is president of the Legal Aid Society.

"Maybe not with Simon around," I said. "Simon's our trusted shop steward."

"You're *all* in on this?"

"Not yet. The other attorneys don't even know about it yet. But when they hear about it, what do you think they'll do?"

"Oh, *man!*" Fischer said, shaking his head, not smiling anymore.

"Right again," I said.

I waited a couple of seconds and let Fischer think it over.

"Tell me something," I said. "What do you think the reaction of the ADAs will be?"

"That's just what I was thinking. Some of them are gonna wish they were Legal Aids, just to get in on it."

"They don't have to be Legal Aids to get in on it."

"You really think it's gonna take off like that?"

"Well, what do you think?"

Fischer shrugged and twisted and squirmed and shook his head. "It could happen," he said.

"Do you think I'm doing the wrong thing, Dave?"

"I can't really say I do. I guess it had to happen. You may have a lot more people on your side than you think."

"By the time this is over I wouldn't be surprised if we even had a judge or two, or three."

That afternoon the word started getting around, and more attorneys than usual came in to sit in the spectator section. They wanted to see if it was really true. I tried not to look at them, just to act natural. But every time I came back in through the pen doorway and said, "Ready for trial," I couldn't miss the smiles and whispers in the front rows.

Late in the day, when some of the other parts had wrapped up, I saw Susan and Simon out there with a few of the other Legal Aids and some ADAs. A great rush of pride and purpose swept through me, and I realized I hadn't felt that particular sensation since the last time I won a murder trial.

Bianchi guessed I'd filled Fischer in. When one of my clients turned down nine months for a heroin sale, he said to Fischer, "What do you think about all this, Dave?"

Fischer and I were both at the bench, resting our arms on the railing.

"Well," Fischer said, doodling with a pen on Bianchi's blotter, "I don't know. I can see Al's point. Let's face it, Judge, sooner or later something had to happen. The whole system really is fucked up, Judge. A lot of people are getting hurt."

Bianchi didn't answer. Just a little nod. "Let's get going," he said. "At least we can get through the calendar."

I felt a little bad for Bianchi. I knew Rhein would be

calling him tomorrow, yelling and screaming, and Bianchi would have a tough time making him understand why there hadn't been more guilty pleas.

When we'd recessed and I took the files back down to the office, Simon and some of the young lawyers were waiting for me. Simon shook my hand and said some trite things about doing the right thing.

"I'll be with you tomorrow," he said. "A lot of us will be with you. And if they try to pull you out, they'll have to pull us all out." He was beside himself with delight, the joyful anarchist on the eve of action, bombs abuilding in the basement.

I left with Susan and was happy to get away. We had a few drinks, waiting for it to get late enough for dinner. I started to relax. The afternoon had been much harder than the morning. Not because of the other attorneys in the audience, but because I had had to push a couple of times, had had to go further, a lot further, than I wanted to. A lawyer is a predictor, really, a prophet. He says to a client, because this and this is true, and since this and this might be true, then your alternatives are such and such, and here's what's most likely to happen. But he lets the client make the actual decision of what to do. I don't like *telling* a client what to do, unless it's clearly in his best interests and he's just too stupid to see it. But that afternoon I told a few clients what to do, and it was *not* in their best interests. They could have copped out and hit the street. I told them not to. That went against everything I'd been doing for years, and it was disturbing. There was this young white junkie, from New Jersey someplace, in for attempted murder, and he really wanted out. He was filthy and emaciated and sick and half crazy and all he wanted was out. He could have got out, too. He was the first one who wasn't making it easy on me, who wasn't some wise guy who made it easy by yelling about how innocent he was. I thought, "So what's it matter if this one guy cops out? One guy all day."

But it couldn't work that way. I looked at that drug-wasted collection of hair, rags, and filth, and I said, "Don't plead."

And he trusted me. He didn't plead.

It was so simple. Revolution with a phrase. No anarchists' bomb. No assassin's bullet. No complicated plot, conspiratorial underground, stockpiled weapons. Just two words. "Don't plead." So easy. And it got easier all afternoon.

We went to dinner and Susan was very quiet, just listening to me talk. Later she said it was like I was high. I could feel the tension draining out. Much more than the tension of the day. I felt as if I'd just confessed to some horrible crime I'd been hiding for half my life, as if I'd been running and hiding and terrified of capture every minute, and now at last it was out in the open. Whatever happened now, good or bad, it was what had to happen. I felt cleansed.

After dinner Susan went back to the apartment with me. Since our weekend in the country she had practically been living there. I wanted her to move in, and I suggested it to her once. I wasn't going to say it to her more than that. I just wanted her to know I wanted her. She was moving slowly. When she was ready, she'd do it.

The next morning went the same as the first. Except

97

that now I'd been joined by about a third of the other Supreme Court attorneys in the Legal Aid's criminal branch. That's more than twenty-five lawyers, citywide, and they were blocking a lot of guilty pleas.

One of the rebels was Susan. She was unlucky enough to be assigned to Judge Niebauer's part. Niebauer was a political hack of such towering stupidity and incompetence that it was said even the Mafia wouldn't use him. Along toward the end of the morning, when Susan had blocked about twenty guilty pleas, she heard him say something to the bridge man about "that smartass broad." She shot back something about a moronic fascist. He fined her two hundred dollars for contempt and threw her out of court.

The chief of the criminal branch went up and smoothed Niebauer's feathers and got the fine withdrawn.

I had been hoping Susan wouldn't get involved. I didn't think she really understood where her involvement might take her. I had told her that in the apartment the previous night, and she had exploded. I couldn't have said anything more incendiary.

"You don't think I can do *anything*," she yelled at me. "You don't even think I'm a person. To you I'm some kind of a *machine—*"

"Some kind of a machine." It had been a strenuous day and I didn't want a fight.

"I'm an—*apparatus*. All you care is that I function properly. If I don't, you give me a couple of kicks, pull out my plug, turn it around, stick it back in . . ."

"Pull out your *what*?"

She was furious. I tried to laugh it off and make up,

but she was too angry. She sat in the living room and didn't come to bed until I was asleep.

It was in the office at lunchtime that Susan told me about her dispute with Niebauer. She was still going on about it when I got a call from Bianchi. He wanted me to come up to his chambers. That didn't surprise me.

"I just had a call from Rhein," he said when I walked in. "He's seen the calendar report from yesterday and he thought it had to be a mistake. We had seventy-seven cases and only nineteen guilty pleas, all private attorneys."

Bianchi stopped talking for a minute. He was standing up about to go to lunch, and I had not sat down. "I just wanted you to know, Al, that the wheels have started to turn. He's very angry. He said some things about you that weren't very nice. He said he was calling Billings."

"Thanks," I said. "I appreciate your telling me. No one knows I'm here and no one will."

He went to the door and stopped with his hand on the knob. "I don't know where this is going to end, Al. I'm still not convinced you know what you've started."

"I know."

I was sorry I hadn't put more force into the words.

Things moved fast. By that afternoon the news reporters had wind of what was happening and were sitting in court. The next day, Wednesday, *The New York Times* had a small story buried inside the second section saying guilty pleas had dropped 33 percent in the past two days and that certain defense attorneys were encouraging clients to demand trials.

Wednesday evening, Rhein invited the Manhattan DA and the president of the Legal Aid Society to his chambers. The result of that meeting was apparent the next morning before court when the chief of the Legal Aid criminal branch assembled all the attorneys and warned them against encouraging not guilty pleas. He swept all the junkies, stickup men and other clients out of the office bullpen area, closed the door, and with all the attorneys standing around leaning on desks and file cabinets he said, "Now, I would not suggest for a moment, and I certainly am *not* suggesting, that clients be encouraged to take guilty pleas when there is not a clear admission of guilt. But I want to remind all of you of the equal gravity of influencing clients arbitrarily to plead not guilty when they do admit guilt, and when it is clearly to their advantage to plead guilty. Not all of us like plea bargaining, but, as they say, it's the only game in town and it will be with us for quite a while. So we must all adjust to it. I caution you against attempting to obstruct the normal flow of justice in the courts. That's all."

He turned toward the door. Jeff Simon, who perhaps by design was at the far end of the room, shouted, "Sir? Excuse me. May I ask a question?"

"Certainly."

"Can you tell us what will happen if these not guilty pleas should continue to, ah, proliferate?"

Some of the other lawyers laughed.

"I have spoken with the Presiding Justice and with the District Attorney. Plans have been made to staff the courts, if necessary, with attorneys assigned by the Appellate Division."

Scattered boos. The meeting ended. The AD frequently assigns private lawyers to represent indigent defendants, for example when two men commit a stickup together and it would create a conflict of interest for both to be represented by the Legal Aid Society. So the threat to replace all LAS attorneys with AD attorneys carried the weight of possibility. It would not be easy to field that many lawyers on short notice, but it could be done. Simon stood up on a desk—he really loved his role—and said, "You all heard the threat, and you all know what's at stake. Each man will do what he feels must be done. As for me, I'm beginning to like the ring of those three little words— *Ready for trial!*"

Good-natured cheers, and we went to court.

Many of the young attorneys were reacting to the—what should I call it? project? crusade?—with happy camaraderie. It was amusing, a change from the routine—for some, a prank. Later in the day that lighthearted attitude disappeared with the first report of violence.

A black man named Russell Benoit was offered time served on a charge of receiving stolen property. He had a private lawyer who naturally advised him to take the plea. He took it and was returned to the Tombs to collect his belongings and go through the release procedure. An hour later he was found on his bunk, beaten unconscious. The news filtered into court at about four o'clock. The next morning the *Times*, on page one this time, said the man was in the intensive care section of Bellevue, in a coma, and that if he lived he would be paralyzed from the neck down.

The *Times* had asked a number of people if the beating was connected in any way with the sudden increase in not guilty pleas. Though almost all the answers, at least from public officials, were negative or evasive, the implication was clear.

To me it was more than an implication. Benoit's cell location was 8-Lower B-6. The eighth floor was about one-third occupied with so-called "heavy" cases, many of them inciters of last winter's riot. Oscar Butterfield was there. His cell location was 8-Lower B-9.

On Friday, all inmates coming to court were told to bring their belongings with them. They arrived in the detention pens like an army of refugees, laden with old boxes, torn bags, bundles of clothes tied up with string. The previous day's warning—threat, if you like—to the LAS attorneys had not worked, and today the lawyer in Part Four was replaced by an attorney assigned by the Appellate Division. It was no more than a gesture. The PJs were fully aware that large-scale replacement would call further public attention to the gravity of the problem, and would almost certainly arouse protests from liberal attorneys highly placed in influential firms.

Even the replacement of the LAS attorneys in a single part was not without problems. The Assistant DA there, a bright young redhead named Collins, balked at working with the new man. He had built a long relationship with his LAS colleague, and loyalty compelled him to protest the replacement. Also, he liked what the LAS lawyers were up to. His offers came higher than they'd been in two years, and his manner was less than cordial.

Actually it made little difference how high the offers were. The defendants by then had started to refuse guilty pleas even without encouragement from their lawyers. They were frightened. And their fear was not greatly diminished by the knowledge that if they copped out they would be released directly into the street without a return to jail. These were street people, and they knew the power and brutality of the street. They were not convinced, not at all, that carrying their belongings to court would immunize them against whatever punishment awaited.

They were correct, of course.

I was standing in the sun on the courthouse steps, talking to Fischer, waiting for Susan to come along for lunch. Fischer was telling me what he'd heard about Collins giving everyone a rough time in Part Four.

"He wouldn't go any lower than three years on a drug sale," Fischer said. "And the judge says, 'Hey, Red, you haven't by any chance joined the Legal Aid Society?' And the AD man says, 'I won't even convey that offer. Anything over eighteen months is unreasonable.' Like he's an expert, right? And he hasn't even been *in* a courtroom for ten years. So Collins gets pissed off and he says, 'Listen, stupid, anything over a *year* is unreasonable. I'm a very unreasonable guy. If your man wants—' "

A woman walking past me toward the street turned and said, "Oh—" I thought she'd remembered something and was turning to go back into the court building.

Then an old man on the sidewalk yelled, "Hey!" and started running up the block.

I looked where he was headed and saw three blacks kicking something in the middle of the sidewalk.

Fischer turned and saw it too, and yelled, and we ran down the steps toward the blacks. They threw in a few more kicks and then sprinted toward Canal Street and disappeared.

A middle-aged man in a white sport shirt was doubled up on the sidewalk. He was groaning, holding his crotch, and blood was running onto his shirt from his face and neck. I looked around for Fischer and saw him at the corner on a police phone.

I bent over the man. He looked up at me and said, "Please, please don't hurt me no more."

Pain glinted in his eyes. He could hardly talk.

"I won't hurt you," I said. "You're all right now. The men who hurt you have left. An ambulance is on its way."

Behind me a voice said, "Leave him alone. That's enough now. Okay, now leave him alone."

I stood up.

A tall man in a business suit put down his attaché case and kneeled next to the man. "Just lie back and relax," he said. "An ambulance is coming."

I stood there feeling accused, and then there were about forty other people pushing in around the man, with more running up. I looked for a cop but didn't see one. Then I heard a siren, and in about fifteen seconds, less than half a minute, three radio cars drove up. Fischer showed his badge to the cops and I knew he'd be talking to them for half an hour so I walked up to Canal Street and got a sandwich.

I was afraid I knew why the man had been attacked. When I got back to the office I called Fischer. The man was a defendant on bail, charged with kidnapping, assault, and rape. He'd abducted an eleven-year-old girl seven years ago. The girl was eighteen now and married, the parents were sick of court, two of the investigating officers had retired and left the city. The ADA made an offer to dismiss everything but assault and accept a sentence of one year. The man took it. He'd been in the Tombs ten months before his wife made bail for him, so he had a walk. He didn't read the papers and he didn't know anything about the dangers of pleading guilty.

Bianchi had said there'd be blood, and I had known there'd be blood. I'd thought about that yesterday when the man was beaten up in the Tombs. But this one today hit me much harder. I'd seen this one. The man's earlobe had been ripped loose. I couldn't get the sight of that out of my mind.

That evening Rhein and the other PJs called another meeting. When it was over Bianchi telephoned me and I met him in a restaurant in Chinatown a few blocks from court. I think he wanted to keep me abreast of the kind of trouble I was causing. Or maybe he was trying to protect me. Anyway, he said the District Attorneys from New York's five boroughs had been at the meeting, plus the president of the New York Bar Association, the Commissioner of Correction, the Police Commissioner, and the president of the Legal Aid Society. Bianchi himself had been invited because it was in his part that the whole mess started. The only other judge there was Richard Malizard, in whose part the young ADA, Red Collins, had balked at seeing the LAS lawyer replaced.

Bianchi told me they were very concerned about Collins because they wanted to replace all the LAS lawyers the next day and they were afraid the replacement would touch off a strike by the ADAs. Bianchi and Malizard, the only two men at the meeting who actually worked in the courts, said that a strike would not surprise them. This incensed the DAs, of course, who said that such a thing was impossible, that their men would never strike.

Bianchi said to me, "Of course the whole matter of replacing LAS lawyers and ADAs was academic because none of the defendants was willing to plead guilty anyway. I told them that. I said, 'As long as you've got released defendants assaulted on the streets it won't matter who staffs the courts or if they're staffed at all. You're not going to get guilty pleas.'"

As he spoke to me, Bianchi kept glancing over at three Chinamen eating at a table in the back. I smiled to myself, wondering if he really thought they might be spies from Rhein's office.

Bianchi said the Correction Commissioner told the rest of the meeting that the city jails were already feeling the pressure. Almost every cell had three men in it, and on one floor in the Tombs they'd put mattresses on the "flats," locked recreation and eating areas around the cells.

"But we can't keep that up," he had said. "Other inmates walk on the mattresses and the men's clothes and that starts fights. If we keep inmates on a twenty-four-hour-a-day lock-in in their cells so they can't trample over the men sleeping on the flats, then we get fights in the cells. We're in a terribly dangerous situation. I'm expecting a riot any minute. Where can we put these men? Another thing. The officers in there see how bad it is and a lot of them—more and more of them every day—are sympathetic with the inmates. You have to be sympathetic when you see the conditions in there. Just the stink. You ought to go over there, your honor."

This last was directed at Rhein, who would be on the moon before he visited the Tombs.

The three Chinamen left. Bianchi watched them until they disappeared past the windows.

Someone at the meeting had suggested taking a handful of defendants and giving them fast trials and maximum sentences. "When the others see a few guys go away for twenty years they won't be so fast to turn down a two-year offer."

Bianchi said he pointed out to the meeting that in the weeks it would take to conclude all of those trials, the inmate population would be so high they'd have to lodge them in Madison Square Garden.

"Then some genius said why not take all the light cases and reduce their bail to fifty dollars. I told them, I said that that would work great for a few hundred men. After that they'd be into the heavy hitters, the homicides and Robbery Ones. You can't release them on low bail and ever expect to see them again."

In the end, they decided to go ahead the next day and substitute Appellate Division attorneys for all the LAS men. At the same time they'd have other lawyers sworn in and ready to take over as ADAs. Other than that, they would do nothing. They would hope.

"This thing can't go on forever," Rhein had said. "It's a temporary crisis, and if we hang on and wait it out, we'll be back to normal in a few days."

The Police Commissioner said he'd put men around the court buildings in all boroughs and that that ought to reduce assaults. Someone suggested that if the cops would simply stop arresting people there wouldn't be any more problems.

Everyone laughed.

■

The cadaverous psychiatrist was back this morning. I glanced up and found him watching me through the bars. I don't know how long he had been there. He looked at me sitting naked on the bunk with pencil and paper, more papers spread out around, and he seemed to think that that alone was sufficient evidence of madness.

Two guards let him in.

"Forget it," I said. "I'm still not crazy. If I get crazy, I'll let you know."

He smiled, leaning against the wall. "Well, you certainly look a little mad sitting there naked with writing paper all over you."

"The present will pass, but the past is with us always."

He nodded sagely. "I understand."

"You don't look so healthy yourself, doctor. You could use a few solid meals. I hear bad eating habits are a sign of emotional disturbance. Like insomnia and impotency."

"Hmmmm."

"Do you know Dostoevsky? 'Shutting somebody else up in a lunatic asylum doesn't prove your own sanity.'"

"Of course not."

He wasn't any fun. I wanted to get back to the writing.

"Look, Doctor, you're wasting your time. I am completely, totally, absolutely sane. There is nothing wrong with me."

"I agree with half of that. You are completely sane. I would say, in fact, that you are abnormally sane. We have a therapy program for that."

"For *abnormal* sanity?"

"It is possible to be too sane."

"You are ridiculous."

"But I am not locked up. See what I mean?"

SIX

A WEEK LATER the court building looked like a fortress under siege. I came out of the subway on Canal Street, and within a block of court I had to show my LAS identification card to police manning barricades. It was the same at the other criminal court buildings in Queens, the Bronx, Brooklyn, even Staten Island. Network television crews were waiting around to film battles between cops and anyone trying to intimidate defendants.

But there were no defendants. The whole scene was a joke, typical of what had been happening for years. Don't repair what's wrong, just put on a show. I knew there wouldn't be any assaults or scuffles, and so did all the other LAS lawyers and ADAs and judges. All the thugs in New York couldn't do the intimidation job as well as those cops. What defendant would take a look at that police firepower and not gain a forbidding respect for the threat it was there to control? "Man, if it takes *that* many cops to keep 'em from kickin' the shit outa me, they must be *big*! I ain' gonna mess with *them!*"

The joke outside the building was nothing compared to what was going on inside. One set of private attorneys assigned by the Appellate Division was representing defendants. Another set had been sworn in as ADAs. Few on either side had any idea what they were doing. At one point a man charged with three counts of first degree murder was mistaken for a daytime burglar and offered two months. He turned it down. His lawyer yelled at him. The judge told the lawyer to shut up. The substitute ADA, discovering his mistake, screamed, "It's off! It's off! It doesn't count!" The spectators howled with laughter. Finally the judge recessed the court and left the bench shaking his head in sorrow and disbelief.

By lunchtime, three judges—including Bianchi—had called Rhein's office to say that if some order could not be restored by the end of the day, they would refuse to sit the following morning.

I moved from part to part watching the chaos. At about noon one of the LAS secretaries found me and said I had a message from the Tombs that one of my clients was demanding to see me and making a big fuss about it, threatening to start a riot unless I came over.

The client, of course, was Oscar Butterfield.

I had to show my ID card to get through cops around the Tombs. Inside, the security was tighter than I'd ever seen it. Usually you show your card through a window, they open the front door, you sign in, go through a locked, barred gate and wait on a bench till your client is brought to the adjoining counsel room, the room with the little cubicles. This time I was searched inside the front door, an officer signed in for me, carefully noting my name and identification number from the ID card, and then escorted me directly to a cubicle in the counsel room. He stood there watching me.

Oscar arrived in handcuffs with three officers carrying

batons. They took off the cuffs, put Oscar in the cubicle, and waited across the room while we talked.

Oscar smelled like a year of sweat. He tossed a piece of candy into his mouth and grinned at me. "How're we doin'?"

"They said you threatened to riot unless I came over here. What's happening?"

"What's *happenin'*? Man, what *ain't* happenin'? This place's packed up like one of them oldtime slave ships. I gotta know what's comin', man. I heard your name on the radio, said you was the lawyer started it all, not lettin' no one plead guilty. I thought about that, what you said last time you was here, and I see your point. But where's it goin', man, what you got in mind? 'Cause a lot of those guys up there, like they do what I tell 'em, you know? But I gotta know myself. We're gonna have a riot here."

"I don't know what's going to happen, Oscar. But I can guarantee you that whatever it is, it'll leave you all better off than you are now."

He slammed the candy around. "You all? Who you mean, you all?"

"All the defendants."

"I ain't *interested* in all the defendants, man. Nobody up there ain't interested in all the defendants. Things are bad up there. Things ain't bad for you. You know what I mean? Ain' nobody up there lookin' to fix nothin' 'cept themselves. The worse things get, the harder it is makin' everything go my way, you know what I mean? We gotta see what we're gettin' out of it."

"What do you want out of it, Oscar?"

"Out."

"Well, maybe that's not entirely impossible. The worse

things get, the more chaotic everything gets, the more chance there is that anything's possible."

He stared at me.

"Look, Oscar. I can't tell you what's going to happen. I'm not a fortune-teller."

He came down hard on the candy, crushed it, sucked the fragments, and popped in another piece. He looked angry. Oscar Butterfield angry is the stuff of nightmares.

"Don' get too big," he said. "You're a lawyer, people say you started it, maybe people on the outside gettin' scared of you. Ain' nobody here scared of you. People here is scared of me. If we start pleadin' guilty again, your whole great motherfuckin' idea is finished, everything goes back to where it was at before."

"That's not true, Oscar. You haven't been to court lately. The courts are paralyzed. They've fired all the Legal Aid lawyers and they've fired all the ADAs and a few of the judges have quit. It won't change anything if the defendants start pleading. So don't get too big."

He leaned his hulk across the table until his beard was in my face. It stank like garbage. I'd have moved my chair back but there wasn't room.

"They got three men in every cell," he said, speaking slowly. "Some cells, they got four men. One on each bunk, two on the floor. That don't leave much room for the mice. We in a twenty-four-hour-a-day lock-in. They got blankets on the flats—twenty, thirty, forty men on the blankets. We got two meals a day, both cold. No showers. A fight starts in your cell, you climb the walls, gettin' out of it. They're makin' knives outa bedsprings and ain't no officers around to take 'em off you. This mornin' they had a fight on the flat in D section and The Man don't go in to break it up. He'd been killed if he went in. They gassed the whole section and took two of the fighters out. They coulda been dead. I don' know. They—"

"Oscar, I—"

He put his arms straight up over his head and brought them crashing down like hammers on the wooden table. An officer rushed to the door, baton raised. Oscar didn't even look at him. His eyes were glued to my face.

I said, "That's all right, officer. We're just discussing his case. There's no problem."

The officer lowered his baton and backed away.

"They coulda been dead," Oscar continued as if nothing had happened. "I don't know. You know what Obso is? Obso's where they keep the crazy men. They never double up in Obso. You put two crazy men together they kill each other. Yesterday, they doubled up in Obso. No one got killed. I wondered about that, and now I got it figured out. Drugs. They got 'em all medicated. They lyin' in there like zombies. Lunch today, I don' drink the coffee. I figure, they medicate Obso, they gonna medicate everyone. I don' wanna be stacked up in a cell like no zombie. I told a few people, don' drink the coffee. We'll see. Maybe tomorrow we got a bunch of sleepy prisoners. I figure if we do, then that gives me that much more power. Me an' my friends. The people who don' drink the coffee."

He stopped. I waited to make sure he was finished.

"Oscar," I said, "I will tell you everything I know. I know that the population of all the city jails is increasing

117

by hundreds of men a day. I know that there are only two ways to stop that increase. One is to stop the input. The other is to increase the output. You got me?"

He nodded, not chewing or sucking or banging. He was all concentration.

"The only way to stop the input is for people to stop committing crimes, which isn't going to happen, or for the police to stop arresting people who commit crimes, which isn't going to happen either. The only way to increase the output is for defendants to start taking guilty pleas again, which looks very, very unlikely, at least for the time being, or for the courts to release the inmates, to just turn them loose and let them go, and that's not going to happen either. So you see that there is no way the increase in the jail population is going to be halted. That's all I know. That's all I can tell you."

"Well I can tell you somethin'," he said. "If there ain't no way to halt the increase, there ain't no way to halt a riot. An' this riot ain't gonna be like the last one. Last time, they had two hundred and fifty men on a floor with three officers. This time we got six hundred men on each floor, and we still got jus' three officers. So you know who this jail belongs to. When we wanna take it, ain't no one gonna stop us, and we gonna take all the officers along with it. You understand? And a lot of those officers, a lot of them, they's on our side, they's *already* on our side, you know that? Last time we took seven hostages. This time, *everybody's* gonna be a hostage. The guards, the inmates, everybody. Ain't nobody gettin' off. So let's just say this riot is gonna be a little more *complicated* than the last one, you know what I mean? An' a little more bloody."

"Why are you telling me this, Oscar?"

" 'Cause I figure maybe you'd like to know. And I figure maybe there's some people you'd like to tell."

I walked out feeling frightened and exhausted. I didn't want to have to be around for that riot. I didn't want to be around for any of it.

Outside the Tombs I saw Fischer across the street next to an ice-cream cart. He was eating a lemon ice.

"You want something?" He nodded toward the cart.

"No, thanks."

"What's happening?"

"I was inside seeing a client."

"I thought you were maybe inciting a riot."

"It's bad in there. My client says they're packed in like slaves. He thinks they're putting drugs in the coffee."

"Good idea. They'd better come up with something."

He started walking slowly to the corner. I told him I wanted to get back to the office.

"Wait a second. You've got a lot of time. Walk up here with me."

So we strolled along, past the uniformed cops and wooden barricades.

"You looking for something?" I said.

"No. Let's just take a walk. It's a nice day."

We got to the corner and turned left and walked along while Fischer licked his lemon ice.

"How's Susan?" he said.

"Fine."

"You seeing a lot of her?"

"Yeah. I see her quite a lot. Why?"

"Nothing. I just wondered."

He took my arm and started across the street. "Let's walk over here."

"Where the hell are you going?"

"No place. Just walking. What's she think of this whole thing?"

"She thinks it's something that had to happen. Why don't you ask her? Look, I've got to get back to the office."

"You can wait a few more minutes. Let's go this way."

He crossed the street again and turned right at the corner. We were away from the Tombs and the court building now and the number of cops had thinned out. He stopped in front of an Italian tailor shop.

"You gonna buy a suit, Dave? What's all this wandering around?"

"Just getting some sun. It's a beautiful day."

We got up to the corner and stopped and he took a deep breath and stretched and turned his face up to the sun.

"Trying to get a tan?"

"Don't be racist, Al, just 'cause I'm trying to get you out and push a little healthy exercise on you. This way."

We turned the corner again. Then he said, "By the way, did you know you're being followed?"

"Not really." I thought he was joking.

"They picked you up when you came out of the Tombs. When we get to the corner we'll turn around and start back and they'll be across the street half a block ahead."

We did, and they were—two middle-aged men in dark business suits.

"Who do you think they are?" I said.

"Don't ask me. You know what you've been up to better than I do."

"I haven't been up to anything."

"Not much. Just wrecking the courts."

"You think they're city cops?"

"Maybe. Or FBI, CIA, IRS, Army Intelligence, State Police, Mafia, White House."

"They're not following me," I said. "I think they're after you."

"No. I saw them outside the Tombs and wondered who they were. When you came out, they picked you right up and they've been with us ever since. I don't know what they've got in mind, but obviously it has something to do with the court situation. Unless you've been smuggling junk or something. Right now a lot of people would like to see you hang. Probably they're keeping tabs, keeping you in sight in case someone wants you for something. Be careful where you go. Don't do anything that could look incriminating. And your phone will be wired, too, so be careful what you say. And if they've taken the trouble to wire your phone, they've tricked the circuit to make the mouthpiece an open microphone, even when it's hung up, so be careful what you say around your apartment. Other than that, you've got absolutely nothing to be concerned about."

Fischer was right. When I went home that night, the two men were still with me. I went out to dinner with Susan, and a different pair tagged along behind us across the street. I didn't tell Susan, but every time I glanced around, there they were.

I was naïve enough not to be worried. I hadn't broken any laws, and I was not about to break any. I had nothing I wanted to hide. They could follow me everywhere, listen to all my conversations, sift through everything in my apartment, and they wouldn't discover so much as an unpaid parking ticket. So I looked on them less as a threat than as an interesting curiosity. As I said, I was naïve.

In the next two days conditions grew more chaotic: no guilty pleas, packed jails, cops surrounding the court buildings, even a few assaults in Harlem, Bedford-Stuyvesant, and the South Bronx on bailed defendants who'd gone to court and pleaded not guilty. Bianchi and two other judges walked out of court and did not return. Others threatened to do the same. The news media were enraged, or pretended to be. Everyone was yelling bloody murder that something had to be done. But no one knew what. A lot of people thought they knew, but they didn't. They didn't know the answer because there was no answer. No one said, "You know, it really appears that this time we've simply had it." But that was the truth.

As usual, the anger and concern presented by the media failed to be anything more to the general public than entertainment. People read the papers and watched the TV news shows, and then went about their business. Few of them knew or cared very much about the courts and the jails. To most people the whole problem was as distant as Southeast Asia.

And then the president of the Patrolmen's Benevolent Association went on television with an extraordinary accusation. I had taken Susan into Carlo's for a drink after court. We were sitting in a booth when some men at the bar looked at their watches and said something to the bartender, who walked over and turned on the TV. An announcer was talking about a special press conference scheduled by Bob Talrich, president of the PBA.

Three men walked in and took the booth next to ours. One of them smiled at me, said hello, and looked over at the TV set. "Started yet?"

"Not yet," I said, guessing he meant the press conference.

"Who's that?" Susan whispered to me.

"Henry Dunlop, warden of the Tombs."

She stared at him like he was something in a cage.

"Come on," I said. "He's not Adolf Eichmann."

"I don't understand how anyone can do that. Just looking at him gives me the chills."

"Actually he's a very nice guy."

"He's a pig."

"You don't even know him. Don't be so hateful. Have a little love for your fellow man."

"Go to hell." The closer we became, the more frequently the fangs appeared.

I leaned across and whispered in her ear. "How can anyone as soft and delicious as you get so mean?"

She shoved me away and aimed her face at the television set.

Talrich came on camera, said good evening, and exploded his bomb. To reduce the steadily increasing pressure within the jails, he said, the police had been secretly ordered to stop making arrests for any crimes other than homicide, rape, robbery, and felonious assault.

He displayed on camera an official piece of police department letterhead called a "49." This particular 49 was marked, "From: Chief Inspector." The Chief Inspector is the highest ranking officer in the department, just below the Commissioner himself, who is a civilian. It was addressed by name to the seven borough commanders with instructions that it was to be hand-delivered to each and was for the eyes and information of no others. The directive ordered these commanders "as prudently and discreetly as possible, and in such manner as to minimize the possibility of external disclosure," to "temporarily eliminate" arrests for any crimes other than those named.

Bob Talrich was a squat, short-tempered, curiously articulate patrolman, and as he sat before the TV cameras he was red-faced with anger. "We are not legislators," he said. "We are not lawmakers. We are merely law enforcers. It is not our purpose nor our right to determine which of those laws legally enacted by elected legislators should be enforced. In a democracy, the people enact laws. The police merely enforce them, equally and uniformly. Only in a police state are police permitted to select the laws they choose to enforce. The patrolmen of the city of New York are shocked at this attempt to impose selective enforcement, to impose police-state methods, upon the citizens of New York."

He spoke slowly, struggling for self-control, each word emerging as if on the end of a taut leather leash. "Who is this order really from? Not from the Chief Inspector, for he would not give such an order without clearance from his superior, the Police Commissioner. Not from the Police Commissioner either, for he would certainly give no such order without clearance from his superior, the Mayor. Let me, then, address the Mayor. Mr. Mayor, by what right do you ask the 30,828 patrolmen in the city of New York to ignore all crimes other than those major felonies named in the directive? By what right do you ask these sworn enforcers of the law to stand by idly in the face of thieves, burglars, forgers, arsonists, drug pushers—"

At this point he stopped speaking and dramatically lifted from the table in front of him a copy of the New York State Penal Code. "Citizens of New York," he said solemnly, "these are our laws. You enacted them. Those which this order permits us to enforce are contained in these pages—" He tore from the book the appropriate pages. He held them towards the camera. They flapped loosely in his hand. "There are eleven pages here," he said.

Then he thrust the rest of the book at the camera. "And this—these are the laws we have been ordered to ignore. To ignore as if you had never passed them. To ignore because the Mayor, the Police Commissioner, the Chief Inspector *say* to ignore them."

Warden Dunlop leaned across the table at one of the men with him, a captain in charge of the court detention pens. "Tough mother," he said.

Susan was watching the screen and Dunlop and the men around the bar. I was watching Susan.

"Citizens of New York," Talrich continued, "I am not the Mayor or the Police Commissioner or the Chief Inspector, and I have no right to countermand their orders. But I am the elected leader of the police patrolmen in this city. And I have today sent to each of them my own directive, and I am repeating to them now its contents, and am now informing the citizens of New York City of its contents. It says simply this: Any patrolman who shares with the Mayor a belief in selective enforcement has the permission of the PBA to report for his assignments and to abide by this directive. And those who do not agree with such police-state practices are encouraged to refuse to cooperate, to refuse to serve, to spend their time instead with their like-minded fellow officers and with their families, searching for some more worthy and democratic answer to the problems that now face us. To every police officer in the City of New York, I say: Search your conscience. Do what you must do."

A tall, heavy cop with a happy red face thrust a fist into the air. "Power to the people!" he roared.

Susan looked from the cop to me.

"Now it'll get exciting," I said. "What do you think?"

"I'm frightened."

"I'd expect you to be delighted."

Dunlop looked around at us. "Heating up," he said.

I wiped my brow. "Hotter and hotter."

Susan and I left, and as we walked past the Tombs toward Center Street, looking for a taxi, she said, "You ought to be in there with the warden and the cops, making dumb jokes."

"Dumb jokes are how you stay alive."

"That's so stupid."

The effect of Talrich's disclosure was explosive. Tens of thousands of listeners—no doubt many of them thieves, burglars, and pushers—telephoned the station, the newspapers, the police, the Mayor's office to ask if the story was true. Callers who got through to the police and the Mayor's office received polite evasions. Those who telephoned the news media were told that yes, the story had been checked and it was indeed authentic.

Now, for the first time, the criminal justice problem was in the laps of individual citizens. Terrified, they locked their doors and brought knives in from the kitchen.

Late that night the Mayor held a televised news conference of his own. I watched it with Susan in my apartment. He said the problem facing the courts and jails was indeed a most serious one, but that his reaction had been blown out of all proportion.

"We do not, have not, and never will attempt to impose selective law enforcement on the people of New York." He spoke without notes from behind the desk in his office. He was jowly, perspiring. His tie was askew, the collar perhaps not buttoned. "The action that has been taken in this particular instance is a temporary measure required to relieve intolerable temporary conditions within our criminal justice system. In no way does it—as some irresponsible individuals have suggested—give carte blanche to criminals. I assure you that crime today, tomorrow, and as long as I am your Mayor, will continue to be dealt with forcefully and with all the legal weapons at our disposal. Have no question about that."

That night only 30 percent of uniformed patrolmen assigned to the midnight-to-eight tour showed up. The next day, the Detectives' Endowment Association and a similar quasi-union of uniformed sergeants endorsed the PBA stand. Only 25 percent of all patrolmen, sergeants, and detectives reported for duty.

The Mayor's measure had been drastic, and showed limited results. Admissions to the city jails dropped from twelve hundred a day to nine hundred a day. Dave Fischer put it just right: "So now instead of drowning in thirty feet of water, we're only drowning in twenty-five feet of water."

By this time the criminal courts had practically shut

127

down. Defendants were not even moved from the Tombs to the court pens. Every morning guards simply went through a list of inmates whose cases would be called that day and asked each man if he wanted to go to court. It saved a lot of needless trouble shuttling inmates back and forth between cells and holding pens.

In the beginning, a couple of foolish inmates had said, yes, what the hell, they'd like to go to court, might be a nice change of scene. They ended up in Bellevue. It no longer mattered if a prisoner pleaded guilty or not, he was beaten merely for going to court in the first place.

Two days after the Mayor's press conference I walked into my office and six reporters jumped me. They wanted to know if I was going to the Tombs.

"I don't know what you're talking about," I said. I'd been in the building three minutes. I hadn't spoken to anyone.

"There's a riot in the Tombs. A prisoner named Oscar Butterfield says he wants you there."

I put some magazines I was carrying on the desk and took my jacket off. My shirt was soaked with sweat. We'd been in a heat wave for three days, temperatures in the high 90s. "When did this happen?"

"An hour ago."

I was wondering what had kept him. I hadn't had the courage to take the responsibility of coming right out and suggesting to Oscar that he initiate a riot, but I knew it would happen sooner or later if conditions didn't improve.

"He says you're his lawyer."

"Well, that's a confession a lot of my clients wouldn't like to make."

128

"He says he wants you in the Tombs."

The reporter doing the talking was a tall, thin, neatly tailored man named Fletcher Wilkins. He was court reporter for the Associated Press. I'd known him for years.

"What else does he want? Fort Knox? A seat on the Supreme Court?"

"He's demanding amnesty, and a TV film crew, and you. He says he needs legal representation."

"I'm flattered by the vote of confidence, particularly in view of the fact that he happens at the moment to be in jail. And no one could quarrel with his recognition that he needs legal representation. Has he killed anyone yet?"

The reporters told me what they knew about what had happened—that a group of prisoners led by Oscar had seized two floors and taken several guards hostage.

"So are you going?" the man from the *Times* asked. He was old and rumpled and overbearing.

"I haven't been asked. I'm certainly not going because the *Times* tells me I've been asked."

And then, on cue, the phone rang.

I met the warden in front of the court building, and with a handshake but no words we walked quickly around the corner to the Tombs. We moved through the police barricades and then through twenty or thirty correction officers milling silently around the entrance. They stared at the warden but did not speak.

Inside we were shoulder to shoulder with helmeted men in bulletproof vests carrying batons and gray gas-mask bags. We shoved through them to the warden's office and he closed the door. He sat down behind his desk, took a deep breath and looked at me.

"Dori, I could break your fuckin' ass."

I said nothing. I'd known Henry Dunlop for five years. He was a stocky, red-faced man who maybe drank a bit too much. Sometimes I ran into him during lunch or after court at Carlo's and we had a couple together.

"I know," he said. "You didn't start it. It's been here all along."

I nodded. "What's with Butterfield?"

He took another deep breath, let it all out, and hunched forward over his desk. Twenty-seven years ago he'd been a street fighter in a South Brooklyn youth gang. Then some of his friends got locked up and he got wise and joined the Marines. When he came out, his longshoreman father found him a job on the Brooklyn docks. Then he applied for government jobs, took tests for everything from patrolman to customs agent. The Department of Correction called him on a Tuesday morning, swore him in on Wednesday, and Thursday (he liked to tell the story to his new officers), "There I was on Rikers Island in my blue serge suit with a shield pinned to the lapel. I didn't even get a uniform for two weeks." He went to school nights and ended up with a master's degree in correction administration. He was liked by the officers, and by many inmates, too.

"He's got three officers hostage on eight and he says he wants out."

"I don't blame him," I said.

"I don't either."

He put his hands to his face and rubbed. I guessed he hadn't had much sleep the night before and was regretting it now, knowing how rough things would get in the next few hours or days.

"If it was up to me," he said, "I'd let them all out. I'm a correction administrator, not some fuckin' zookeeper. Twenty minutes ago on the phone I told the Commissioner I was swapping jobs with the guy who runs the Central Park Zoo. He makes more than I do, and even the baboons have six times more square feet per pound than the inmates in this hole."

"So what are you going to do?"

"I'm going to do everything I can. I'm gonna make every concession I can and meet every demand I can. They want you up there? You're willing to go? Fine. They got you. They want a TV crew? Beautiful. They got it. But amnesty? Al, this Butterfield's a nut. How can anyone give them amnesty? That's not even legal."

"Legal becomes what's necessary."

"Al, all I want at this point is to get those officers out of there. We haven't been able to find out anything about them. Butterfield's fighting a war of nerves."

He waved a hand toward the street. "Their wives are out there. And the other officers, the COBA, are coming down all over me." The COBA is the Correction Officers Benevolent Association.

"Since our little party last winter there's been a lot of strong feeling about not negotiating with rioters, just going right in. So I've got some officers who want to charge in, and I've got others who won't go in at all."

"What do you mean, won't go in at all?"

"Oh, yes. You didn't know that? We walked through them coming in. Let me tell you what happened, in a nutshell. Butterfield took the eighth floor. I'm not exactly sure how yet, but I can guess. Anyway, so what? He took it. Then he calls the control room to tell 'em he's got the floor, tell 'em what he wants. The control room captain calls the A officer on ten to alert him, and the idiot says something out loud and a bunch of inmates on the bridge heard it and decided to join the fun. And there went ten. Then word got to the other floors and they started setting fires. Blankets, clothes, mattresses, magazines, newspapers. We've been sleeping men on blankets and mattresses on the flats and they turned the whole fuckin' thing into a fire festival. They stuck the hostages in the back sections and let us up with three-inch hoses. I walked back on a catwalk on ten with an officer and there was so much smoke we couldn't breathe. We soaked the place down through the bars—burning blankets and trash and shit, guys running around naked, men in the cells yelling they're burning to death. It was like hosing down animals in a zoo. A madhouse, Al. One fucking madhouse.

"So we got the fires out and then nine floor officers walked off, handed over the keys to the inmates and walked off. How do you like that? I don't even blame them. If I wasn't warden I'd be out there in the street myself. These guys have to live with all that shit. They're locked up there eight hours a day. I'm not kidding myself they're all a bunch of great humanitarians, but they have to live with it too. Only when they fight back we don't call it a riot, we call it a strike. So then after that we lost seven clerical men and about a third of the receiving-room officers. Right now we've got six officers holding out in the kitchen on the second floor. And we've got the elevators. And we've got the seventh-floor crossover from the jail to the court pens. Other than that, the only secure floor is the one right there under your feet."

He stopped for a second, then remembered something and began again. "Oscar and the other leaders are communicating between floors with the telephones. If we cut the lines, we can't talk to them either. They've got leaders on every floor, and if anyone tells me this wasn't organized, he's full of shit. We've had these Prisoners' Lib guys identified in here for two months."

He pulled out a handkerchief and wiped the perspiration from his face. "That crowd out there in the hall—" he nodded toward the door—"is every warm body I could scrape up, and a few of them I'm not so sure of. Between you and me, the men out there on the street are smarter than the men in the hall. They're the ones who're right. Normally, no. Normally, the best way to combat a disturbance like this is fast and furious. Move quickly with everything you've got. But not this time. Because this time those guys upstairs are right. They're just fucking right and it doesn't take a genius to see it. You wouldn't believe what it was like in here, Al. I mean *before* all this started. You see these guys in the counsel room and court. You should see 'em upstairs. Three in a cell we had even before this. We used to get guys come down here from upstate on appeals, and one of 'em walks in in a neatly pressed suit carrying an attaché case. If he wasn't in cuffs you'd think he was from the Governor's office. And then you stick him in a nine-by-six iron box with two naked blacks been there a year, and he takes a look at them on the bunks and he says to the officer, 'Hey, where's my bunk?' And the officer says, 'You ain't got no bunk, fella, sleep on the floor.' Now there's mice and maybe water and piss on that floor, and this is some heavy hitter doing twenty to life for wiping out a bank someplace, and he's gonna say, 'Oh, okay,' and just lie down? No way, man. You got a problem. Something had to break. So now, today, you can't show that upstairs there to a reasonably intelligent man and have him believe it's right. And what do I do when the guys in the hall wake up too, when the COBA pulls them off? Why the hell should they put up with this shit? The cops saw the light. They struck. The firemen struck. Even the fuckin' sanitation men struck."

He stopped and leaned back in his chair. While he was so talkative I thought I'd try for a confession. "Are they drugged?"

He shot me a look, glanced at the ceiling, then let his body go forward over the desk. "They are."

He looked at his watch. "Or they were. Between us, they had something in their coffee this morning. That was almost four hours ago. They say a fix only goes four hours. I can't tell you the battling that went on around here over that. The thing was this. These floors, the largest of them, were designed for a hundred and twenty men. A long time ago we put in two hundred and forty and learned to live with it. The crowding increased suicides, assaults, and sodomy, but who the fuck cared? As long as things stayed pretty quiet and you didn't have riots, the politicians kept quiet. The public kept quiet. The newspapers did their once-a-year hell-in-the-Tombs story, and that was that. But noise turns everyone into humanitarians. Did you know that? You get yourself a good noisy riot and suddenly the politicians, the press—everyone's a humanitarian. So we lived with two hundred and forty. Then this party of yours started and we went up to six hundred.

Just like that. Zip. Six hundred men on a floor. Still the three officers. Now, let me tell you something. There's no way to hold that many men on one of these floors without drugs. Just no way. Not with three officers, not with thirty. Just NFW, man. No fuckin' *way*. People think you can take steel and concrete and it'll hold anything. They think you can keep jammin' 'em in, jammin' 'em in. What can they do? Where they gonna go? But you take a few hundred of *these* guys, and forget the assaults and the suicides. You give 'em enough time and they'll plain tear the place up. That party last winter they ripped out steel locking devices and broke through reinforced, foot-thick glass bricks. When you get upstairs, take a look at those steel tables bolted to the floor. Those bolts are an inch thick, four of them to each leg. They ripped those legs off the floor, ripped them off the tables, and used them for clubs. They broke off a four-foot-long steel locking handle and scraped an edge on one side and had themselves a machete, a battle-ax."

He put out his hands, palms up, large red longshoreman's hands. "People don't realize the power of two bare hands and rage. Multiplied by six hundred—"

The phone rang and one of those two bare hands picked it up.

"He's here now, Commissioner. He's going up."

He put his hand over the mouthpiece and whispered. "You are going up?"

I nodded.

"Right. Them too. I talked to them an hour ago. The crew should be here now. Right, Commissioner."

Dunlop went up with me in the elevator. I began to

smell it. Dunlop said, "It gets worse. I haven't smelled anything like this since the last time I took a piss in the Port Authority bus terminal."

Then he put out his hand. "We can be on the same side, Al."

"Everyone's on the same side," I said. I was trying not to breathe.

The elevator doors opened and I stepped off into a wall of stench and noise. The heat and the stink of urine and shit, of toilets clogged for days, pressed in around me like syrup. I could taste it. I could feel it in my eyes. The noise was crushing—hundreds of men, sensing freedom, shouting, stomping, pounding, the sound ricocheting off steel, tile, concrete, swelling the floor until you could feel the pressure on your skin.

Halfway across the bridge, in the eye of the storm of stink and noise, I saw Oscar at a desk. He screamed at us.

"Just leave him right there, Warden, and take off."

Dunlop left and Oscar sent a prisoner with a key to unlock the gate and let me in.

The Tombs' eighth floor, like most of the others, was H-shaped. The crosspiece joining the four "sections" was called the bridge. There was a desk there and a phone and each prisoner's floor card. The only alarm was the telephone. If it was left off the hook for ten seconds without a connection, a light went on in the control room downstairs.

I walked over to Oscar. The hostages were sprawled around the desk, gagged, bound hand and foot with torn sheets. They stared at me with fear and pleading. The prisoners sat beside them with knives. All the men—inmates and hostages—were black, and it felt odd to have those dark eyes begging help from me, the only white man.

I'd planned to say something light and casual to Oscar, to let him know I wasn't frightened and wouldn't be cowed. I didn't mind being there to help him, but I wasn't taking orders from him. After one minute on his side of that locked gate I wasn't so sure I could keep my resolve. It was the first time I'd been upstairs in the Tombs. The bridge area—large and deserted except for three hostages, three inmates, and myself—was dim, damp, and eerie, like something underground.

"What do you want?" I said to Oscar.

"You know what I want. I already told the man. I want amnesty."

"You also said you want a film crew."

"Yeah. I want the television up here so's everyone can see what kind of a shit hole they been makin' us live in. Then maybe they understand a little of what this here's all about."

"And what do you want me for?"

"Legal representation. For when they make promises, so we'll know what kinda motherfuckin' shit they tryin' to put on us. And for negotiating. And for whatever I want."

He laughed very loud.

"Look, man," he said, "you on my side, right? Don't look so angry, man. We got a good thing here. We handle it right, it gonna work out real good. You told me that yourself. Stop lookin' so angry and let's get on with things."

"I'll stop looking angry if you'll stop tormenting those officers."

137

"Tormentin'!" He flashed a look at the hostages and prisoners. "Hey, put them knives away. They ain't gonna do nothin'. You just sit there and watch them and keep them knives away."

Then to me, "Ain't nothin' gonna happen to those guards. Don't worry none about them."

Before he could say any more, the elevator doors opened again and four white men in short-sleeved shirts stepped out slowly, tentatively, carrying equipment. The warden was not with them.

Oscar jumped up and went to the gate with the key. One man already had a handkerchief to his face. He was short, slender, early twenties, and had a tape recorder slung over his shoulder. He carried a two-foot-long sausage-shaped microphone. Another man carried a camera, another lights. The fourth man, who carried nothing, introduced himself and the others to Oscar. He said he was the correspondent, the talker. He was a big man himself, but you could see Oscar impressed him, scared him. He looked at that sweaty bald head, at the wiry, filthy beard, the scar, hulk, height—and, yes, you could say Oscar scared him.

Oscar let them onto the bridge and started talking. What a ham he was. He had to shout every word, but he told the whole glorious story of his riot. The lights came on, the camera rolled, the microphone was shoved into his face, and he was a star.

"They call our names out for court, see, and we say, Yeah, man, we wanna go to court, and the officer lets us out to the bridge here and then he goes to unlock the A gate there to the elevators, the gate you jus' come through, and I jus' grabbed the garbage can there and cold-cocked that ol' motherfucker."

He was smiling and laughing, enjoying the story. He might have been another kind of man telling friends how he caught a 200-pound marlin.

"Then my friends there jumped the other two pigs and we all tied everybody up and gagged 'em all. An' then we had this plan, see, where we was gonna take the whole house, the whole jail, so I, we, all of us, eight of us, man, we left Billy here with the pigs here and we took one of the pigs with us and went on up in the elevator to the top, up to eleven where they have the infirmary up there and some lockers and the chaplain's office. And that was sweet, man. We got off that elevator an' we all had knives, and there's this short, fat honky pig sittin' there at the desk, comfortable, man, shirt unbuttoned, tie all folded up real neat on the desk, and he's readin' a magazine."

Oscar and two of his lieutenants laughed at the memory of it. The correspondent laughed, too.

"Now he sees us standin' there outside the A gate with this pig with a knife on him, and he jus' turns white, man, turns *white,* and reaches for the phone. So I press the blade a little right up under my pig's chin, man, an' he goes right up on his toes, man, right up on his *toes.* An' I say, 'Touch that phone, he's dead.' That pig *grabbed* his han' back from that phone, like it was red-hot, man. So I tell him to open the gate. Now he don' like that. He says he can't do that. He says he won't do that. So I jus' give my pig a little nick, a little *nick,* and this trickle of blood runs down his neck. And the pig grabs his keys and he's fumblin' through 'em like mad, man, tryin' to find the key to the A gate. So we tie him up an' leave Carl there with him an' we leave for ten, next floor down. We was gonna go like that through the whole house, take the whole house, but then the pig we got with us, he's still bleedin' and he thinks we really cut his throat, an' he's moanin' and groanin' and then on the elevator he passes out. So we go back to eight to trade him in on a new one an' when we get to eight we figure, hey, man, this is crazy runnin' all over the house like this in this here elevator, we better jus' stick on eight an' eleven, we don' need the whole place nohow, we can do as much with two floors as with the whole thing. So then I call the control room. Down there they don' know nothin' yet, they don' know what's happenin'. And Captain Tupolo answers."

Oscar and his friends laughed. This was gonna be a good part.

" 'Control room. Captain Tupolo.' " Oscar mimicked the voice.

" 'Captain Tupolo,' I say, 'the house belongs to the people.' Then I hang up. Man, he don' know whether shit or go blind. He calls back. I answer it. 'Eighth floor, people speakin'. He says, 'Who this?' I say, 'This here is Oscar Butterfield. Lemme speak to the Dep.' Man, I could hear the alarms ringin' down there all over the place. So the Dep comes on, Deputy Warden Waco—Wacky Waco, crazy, man. He says, 'Who's this?' I say, 'This here's Oscar Butterfield, leader of the Tombs section of the Prisoners' Liberation Army. The house belongs to the people.' He hangs up. Then we all get down on the floor behind the hostages over there, up against the wall, waitin' for 'em to come up. And, man, in two minutes those elevator doors open an' ten pigs with sticks and flak jackets and helmets and gas masks dump outa there, an' we got our knives up to the hostages' throats, an' I yell, 'Man, I'm gonna count ten an' if all you gentlemen ain't back on that bus I'm gonna cut this here throat. An' if you try the gas, that's jus' like you cut the throat your own self.' So they get back on the elevator an' leave, don' say nothin'. Then the phone rings again, only this time it's the warden, we got the warden this time. He says, 'Butterfield, what the hell you want?' I say, 'Out, man.' He say, 'Don't be stupid.' I say, 'Amnesty, man. I want amnesty.' He say, 'Amnesty, what kinda fuckin' amnesty?' He say, 'You outa your motherfuckin' mind.' He say, 'I'm comin' up with keys, alone, no officers, no gas, an' I'm gonna unlock the gates and come in and you and the other inmates are gonna go back in the section jus' like nothin' happened and we can forget this here whole thing. An' you an' me an' anyone else you like can sit down here in my office like men and talk everything over an' if you got problems we'll do what we can to work 'em out.' He says, 'We'll do it like men, and no one'll get hurt, and this whole thing right here now with the hostages will all be forgotten.' "

Everyone laughed and snorted.

"Man, you see, he thought I might was gonna believe that shit. So I say, 'No, man, that's a nice speech, but that ain' what we got in mind. There ain't no way talkin' is gonna work things out. The talkin's over, man, the talkin's through, you know what I mean? Only thing's gonna work now is like I say, man, amnesty.' So then I tell him I want Mr. Dori here, my lawyer, up here, and I tell him I want the TV people."

He stopped talking and waited for the correspondent to say something. The correspondent was a little nonplussed. Finally he said, "Well, could we look around?"

"Sure, man, that's what you're here for."

Oscar unlocked the gate to the elevated catwalk running along A section. He led us onto the catwalk, myself in the rear. We were about four feet above floor level, looking down on the flat, on the tables Dunlop had mentioned bolted to the floor, on blankets and men, and across those men for thirty or forty feet to the cells. The cells were in two tiers, one slightly below the catwalk level, the other slightly above. On the catwalk, we were protected by bars from men on the flat.

The light man switched on his lights, the sound man turned dials, and they started filming. They walked slowly the length of the section. The prisoners jumped up on the tables and danced and waved and shouted. They looked insane and without doubt many of them were. Some were completely naked. One had long hair laced through with colored candy wrappers and narrow strips of sheet. More strips of sheet were tied in criss-cross patterns around his calves and forearms. Another prisoner, a towel wrapped around his waist and between his legs like a bikini bottom, suddenly jerked a blanket up from the floor, swirled it around his shoulders like a cape, and ran to the bars, shouting up at us.

"Man, you gotta come on the flat! You don' see *nothin'* up there. You don' see the cells, man. You gotta see the cells!"

He was right. The light man had been aiming into the cells, but they were too far away. All we could see were arms waving through the bars and dark shapes prowling like animals.

The only way to get close to the cells was to go into the flat. No one wanted to do that. When we were back out on the bridge, Oscar talked to the correspondent. I couldn't hear what he was saying, but it doesn't matter. Oscar walked over and unlocked the gate to the flat and went in alone. He called over three very large black men. They leaned towards him as he spoke, listening with great attention and respect. Those men then moved through the flat, ordering the rest of the prisoners back against the cat-walk, away from the cell row.

Then we moved in, a little parade—Oscar first, followed by the correspondent, the light man, the cameraman, the sound man, and myself.

They aimed the light into the first cell, and a man on the top bunk sat up and yelled, "Hey, man, get that fuckin' thing outa my eyes, man, what you doin'?"

The toilet was broken, and an inch-deep puddle covered the floor and flooded out a few feet onto the flat. A number of other toilets must have been clogged too, for we could see now that the flat was covered with large puddles, some of them more than an inch deep.

Three men sitting on the cell's lower bunk, their bare feet in the puddle, looked up at us like a row of monkeys. All wore undershorts.

"You see what happened," Oscar yelled to the correspondent, "was that usually this here cell, the first one, was left open with no one in it so durin' lockout, when the men in the cells were let out onto the flat here and then their cells locked up again, they'd be able to use the toilet

143

in this cell, this first cell here what was left unlocked. But then the toilet broke so now they use an empty cell at the other end."

No one asked him what these four men used.

As we moved along, getting deeper and deeper into the section, I started getting scared. The fifty or sixty men corralled along the catwalk yelled and waved, and if they wanted to take us they would have no problem. We were five juicy white representatives of the legal-media establishment, and I wasn't too sure Oscar and his friends would fight to save us.

Faces appeared at the bars of almost every cell we passed, and prisoners yelled, "Hey, man, what's this for, this for the TV? Where you from, we gonna be on the TV?"

At one cell a short young black with an Afro yelled to his white cellmate, a skinny half-naked creature who looked about thirteen, "Hey, Mouseman, you on the TV, man."

We stopped and they aimed the light in. They filmed the cell, covered with magazine pictures, and as the cameraman panned around to the right I noticed something else stuck to the wall. It was a small skeleton, maybe a bird. Then I realized it was a mouse, stuck to the wall with blobs of dried white paste. Toothpaste.

"Show 'em, Mouseman," the young black yelled, laughing. "You're on the television, man, show 'em!"

The skinny one who looked thirteen reached under the lower bunk and pulled out a foot-square box and put it on his lap and took off the lid. It was filled with brown mice, about a hundred or more of them, crawling over each other. They were thin and hairless, some chewing on each other. Five or ten pink-skinned babies huddled in a corner.

The cameraman filmed, and we moved on.

We had reached the end of the section, and were just turning to start back, when something flew from a cell and struck the sound man in the chest. Instinctively he put his hand to where it hit, and then drew the hand away, staring at it. It was covered with shit.

"Motherfucker!" a prisoner yelled from the cell. "Motherfucker! Motherfucker! Motherfucker! I'll kill your ass, kill your ass, kill your ass."

The light man swung his light quickly into the cell and we saw another prisoner grab the screaming one and throw him into a corner on the flooded floor. He lay there trembling. "Kill your ass," he mumbled. "Kill your ass, kill your ass . . . your ass . . . your ass . . . your ass. . . ."

They got it all, the sound man recording through a shit-covered microphone, never missing a word. The network showed it that night, language and all, on the Walter Cronkite show.

When we got back to the bridge, and the section gate was locked, Oscar told the correspondent, "Now that's Lower A. There's also an upper tier in A section, and then there's B, C, and D sections, upper and lower, just like A, and then two small sections in the back, E and F."

The correspondent was dripping with sweat. He said, "I think we've got enough."

The sound man had his shirt off and was using the back of it to wipe his hands and equipment.

"But I'll tell you something we would like," the correspondent said. "Could we talk to the guards?"

He hesitated just an instant before calling them guards.

Oscar picked it up. He never gave anyone anything for free.

"Call 'em hostages. We ain't cannibals just 'cause we got hostages. Yeah, you can talk to 'em. Help yourself."

Oscar walked over and pulled the gags off.

The cameraman sat on the floor in front of the hostages, the camera on his shoulder. The correspondent sat next to him. He started with the youngest.

"What's your name?"

The sound man thrust his microphone at the guard.

"William Raleigh." His voice was low and wary, barely audible.

"How do you feel right now?"

"Scared. I don't like having a knife on me and bein' tied up."

"How long have you been a guard?"

"Three months."

"What made you become a guard?"

"It's a job. I go to college part time. This here is a job."

He seemed to have something he wanted to say. The correspondent stayed quiet.

"Can I tell you something? I don't hold nothing against these men. They haven't hurt me yet, and I hope they don't hurt me, but they had the right to do what they did. No one has a right to keep men the way these men've been kept. These aren't just prisoners, these are men. If I was one of them I'd do it, too. When I saw him hit the A officer with the garbage can, I just handed over the keys and said, 'Here, brother, right on, I'm with you.' I don't like havin' a knife on me, and I'll admit I'm scared, but they haven't abused me half as much as this place here

146

has abused me in the past three months since I got here."

"So you're in favor of this, of the riot?"

"Yeah. I'm in favor of it. I'm all for it. If they untie me, I'll take off this uniform and hold a knife in my own hand."

The hostage next to him was nodding and muttering, "Right on. Right on, man."

The correspondent turned to him. "You seem to agree with Mr. Raleigh."

"Yeah, man. Everything he said, that goes for me, too."

"What's your name?"

"Wallace Hoke."

He went on to the third officer. "What's your name?"

"Richard Baker."

He was older than the others and bigger—a thick, stocky body, serious face.

"What do you think?"

"I don't think like them. I been here longer than both of them together. I was a hostage before, they took me hostage in the winter riot, right here on this floor, and the next day I was back. They offered me a transfer to another jail and I said, 'What I want to move for? I see these people on the street, I'm not gonna get away from 'em, I'll stay right here where I am—'"

"Where do you live?"

"Bedford-Stuyvesant."

"Why did you become a guard?"

"We're not guards. We're correction officers."

"Why did you become a correction officer?"

"Same as anybody else. City job. And to see if maybe I couldn't do somebody some good. In the last riot, didn't no one treat me bad, didn't no one say one foul word to

147

me. Because I treat them all like men, and they know it. You're a man. I'm a man. You treat me like a man, I'll treat you like a man. I don't like the way this place is. This is a shit hole. I'm not sayin' it ain't inhuman. But that don't give no one the right to take things into their own hands. You got to do the best you can with what you got, and if what you got ain't much—well, you ought not to take things into your own hands."

"But, brother—" The first hostage, the youngest one, started to speak. The microphone and camera swung toward him.

"I ain't your brother," Baker said without moving his head, staring straight ahead. "Don't call me brother. I got two brothers and one half-brother. You ain't none of 'em."

The correspondent waited a minute, but no one said anything. He stood up, the rest of the crew following him, and turned to Oscar, who was relaxing at the desk.

"What's your feeling? What is it you want?"

Oscar grinned, straightened up in his chair, and proceeded to ramble on for several minutes about inhuman conditions, amnesty, the rights of man, and so forth. He was the engaging jailhouse philosopher. Finally he said, "Justice, man. Justice. Just us. Just us, man."

The correspondent said, "So what it all boils down to then is that all you want is to get a little justice."

Oscar laughed. He was having a ball. "Man, justice ain't somethin' you *get*. Justice is somethin' you gotta *take*."

I smiled, too, impressed by Oscar's rhetoric. The correspondent turned to me. He had a good thing, getting into the Tombs in the middle of a riot, and he wanted every-thing out of it he could get. We were turning into a Sunday afternoon talk show.

"How do you feel about it, Mr. Dori?"

I thought for a second and decided, what the hell, why not be honest?

"It's been my experience," I said, "that when defend-ants say they want justice, what they really want is a free one."

"A free one?"

"Parole. Justice is the last thing they want. It's the last thing any of us wants. Where would any of us be if suddenly we got hit in the back of the neck with justice? How many saints do you know?"

They picked up their gear and got ready to leave. The sound man threw his shit-covered shirt into a garbage can. Oscar yelled at him, "Hey, man, what you doin'? We got enough shit up here. Don't leave none of your shit up here."

The sound man couldn't believe it. He looked at Oscar to see if he was serious. Oscar wasn't, but he looked it. So the sound man retrieved the shit-covered shirt and carried it out with him.

When they were gone, Oscar spoke to a couple of his lieutenants and they took Baker, the older officer, back into C section. I didn't like that.

"Now wait a minute, Oscar."

"Don't worry about nothin'. I ain't gonna hurt him. I ain't no savage. I look like a savage? They just gonna give him a private room. I ain't got nothin' against the man, just takin' some precautions, get his mouth outa the way, put it some place where it can't mess up no right-thinkin' heads."

"I want to see where they put him."

"You want to go in there, you welcome."

He walked over to the C section gate and unlocked it. "Come on, man. You want to go back see where he is, go ahead."

The flat had about sixty men in it, almost all black, standing around in groups and sitting at the tables. The ones nearest the gate heard Oscar and stopped talking to watch me.

Baker and the two inmates were already disappearing into the back of the section. I walked through the gate, moving quickly, eyes straight ahead, trying to look very businesslike and not at all frightened. I caught up with them at the back as they unlocked a gate into E section, a small row of cells running perpendicular to the four main sections.

Oscar's men took four inmates out of a cell, put them on the flat, and locked up Baker. No one said a word.

We walked back to the bridge.

"Okay?" Oscar said. "Happy now?"

I nodded. But I knew that if Oscar started chopping up hostages, Baker would be the first to go.

It was after one o'clock. Inmates had started yelling, *"On the food! On the food!"* It became a steady, pulsating, wall-shaking chant. My head ached. Nausea started.

Oscar turned to me. "What we gonna do?"

"It's your riot."

"You call the warden, tell him if he wants to see his officers alive again, he'd best send up some food. And ask him what he's doin' about that amnesty. I ain't gonna wait forever."

I called Dunlop and relayed the message.

"Al, how are the hostages?"

"The hostages are fine. What about the food?"

"We'll do everything we can. The Commissioner's here in the office with me now. Anything we can do, we'll do. But Al, about the food—there's no way we can feed thirty-five hundred men when we don't control the house. We have to use sentenced help for feeding, Al, we don't have enough officers to handle it, and we can't have inmates moving without control and through the kitchen, which is about all we do control. We'll just end up losing the kitchen, too."

I let that slide for a minute and brought up another problem. I wasn't particularly hungry, but the stink was really getting to me.

"Can't you at least get a plumber up here? This place is knee-deep in shit."

"Al, we've got a plumber working on it. The problem's not on the floors. The problem's in the basement."

"Dunlop, don't bullshit me. These toilets are clogged up here."

"That's not what the plumber says. He says the problem's in the basement. I'm not a plumber, Al. What do I know from plumbing? The man says the problem's in the basement, it must be in the basement. He's down there now."

Oscar had something he wanted to tell me.

"Just a minute, Warden, don't hang up."

"Ask him about the medicine," Oscar said. "This here's

a bi-daily floor. We got men need their medicine twice a day. We got epileptics, people with asthma—"

"Dunlop? The men here want to know what about the medicine. They've got epileptics here and evidently a lot of other inmates who need medication twice a day."

"We're working on that, Al. We're getting it set up with the health people."

I hung up.

"What about the amnesty?" Oscar shouted to me.

"Oscar, he says he can't send up food, and he's bull-shitting about getting the plumbing fixed, and maybe he's bullshitting about the medication, too. So you want to ask him about amnesty, *you* ask him." My head was throbbing. I was afraid I was going to throw up.

He grabbed for the phone.

"He'll get food up here damn fuckin' fast when we start sendin' pieces of Mr. Baker down on that elevator."

"Oscar, wait a minute. Put the phone down."

He was so angry he couldn't dial. His huge fingers slipped out of the holes.

"Oscar, I've got an idea. Listen to me, and then you can still call if you want to. But listen first."

He looked at me, trying to figure if I really had an idea. He put the phone down.

"Why be so eager to get food up here, and the plumbing fixed, and medication? They're doing you too much good, much more good than any violence you start yourself. That's why the film crew was here. And when they show that film there's going to be hell to pay outside. The warden hasn't figured that out yet. After they show that film, he'll be begging you to let food and medicine and plumbers up here. You don't even need a riot. This whole place *is* a riot. After two or three days of no food, no medicine, no cleaning, you get another TV crew up here to film starving inmates wallowing in shit, men throwing fits, and before you know it there'll be a mob in the street trying to tear this place down from the *outside*. Then they'll give you amnesty."

His mood had changed as I spoke. He was beaming.

"But what am I gonna do about them?" He gestured toward the sections, the screaming and pounding. "*On the food! On the food! On the food!*"

"What can they do? Where they gonna go?"

He laughed. "You are some kinduva diabolical son of a bitch." He laughed again and slapped the desk. "And you asked me why I got you up here."

He reached above the desk and flipped the switch on a PA amplifier. He put the microphone to his lips.

"Now listen to me! Listen to me!"

The chanting diminished only slightly, but he continued anyway.

"We got the whole jail. The whole jail is ours. But the pigs got the first floor and the street. So we gonna wait 'em out."

The shouting died down.

"We gonna wait 'em out. If we do that, we'll be outa here in one or two days. So stop the poundin' and the yellin' and take it easy. One or two days we'll all be in the street."

The PA went off and there were random noises around the floor. Then slowly it began again—no cries for food now, but the steady banging, pounding, screaming.

In an hour we had a call from the warden.

"We're still working on the medication, Al. And the plumber says he might be able to get things going in a couple of hours. How are the hostages?"

"They're okay."

"I hope you're doing everything you can."

"Of course."

"Can anyone hear me?"

"No."

"We really need your help, Al. It's getting worse. The other jails are rioting. It's everywhere."

"I'm not surprised."

"I guess I'm not either."

He was quiet, waiting for me to remember to yell about the food.

"Well, okay then, Al, we'll keep doing what we can down here. I'll tell everyone the hostages are okay. We're gonna try to just stick it out, Al, and hope Butterfield and his friends come to their senses. We're counting on you, Al, hoping you can talk some sense to them."

"Right." I tried to give the word a flat noncommittal tone.

When I told Oscar about the other riots, he only nodded. He didn't care about any riot except this one.

At nine that night I said I wanted to check on Baker again.

"Take him in," Oscar said, and a black almost as big as Oscar himself picked up the keys and walked back with me.

Baker was lying on the lower bunk.

"You okay?" I asked.

"I'm okay, man. You look out for yourself."

He had nothing more to say. I went back to the bridge. The racket had subsided, but now there were individual screams for aid. Perhaps they had been there all along, inaudible beneath the general din. Oscar and his men ran from section to section, call to call—stopping fights, calming lunatics, explaining that the food and medication would be available when "the pigs" surrendered.

I wanted another talk with the skinny thirteen-year-old, the mouseman. I'd seen tens of thousands of defendants in my life, but never on their own ground. I'd talked to them in my office, and counsel rooms and court. But I'd never encountered them in their natural habitat, which was the street and the Tombs.

This time I went back alone. The flat and the cells were dark, and many of the men were sleeping on blankets on the tables. I moved quietly, stepping over puddles. I stopped at Lower A-8.

"Hey, man, I thought you left."

It was the young black with the Afro. He was sitting on the lower bunk, nearest the bars. A tall black kid and Mouseman sat next to him. The top bunk was covered with a large man either dead or sleeping. He never moved.

"The TV people left," I said. "I'm still here."

"Who are you?"

"I'm an attorney. Legal Aid."

"Oh, yeah, man, I seen you," the tall one said. "I thought I recognized you. I seen you in court last month."

"What's the charge?" I asked.

"Stickup." He waved his head at the other black. "My brother and me."

His brother, the Afro, said, "What's happenin' here? We gonna get out?"

"I don't know. I hope so. It's possible. We'll know in a couple of days. Who'd you stick up?"

"Not me, man, my brother. I just went along."

"He don' like to work," the brother said. Robbery was work.

"You don't like to work?" I said to the brother.

"No, man."

Both of them laughed, a private joke.

"Why not?"

"He too lazy, man. He say if he ain't eatin', he sleepin', an' if he ain't sleepin', he fuckin', an' if he ain't fuckin', he pissin'. He say he ain't got no time to work."

They were breaking up.

I laughed, too, and looked around. My eyes had adjusted to the dark, and I got a closer look at the cell. Next to one of the magazine pictures was a notebook page with writing on it. I couldn't make out the writing.

"What's that say?" I asked.

The tall black reached for it.

"Hey, man, you better watch out," the Afro said, looking at the bunk above them.

The tall one kept reaching, but with a close eye on the top bunk. He pulled the page off the wall and handed it to me. The back was covered with toothpaste.

In laboriously detailed Gothic script someone had penciled, "Give me a gun, man, and I will blow my own or somebody else's brains out. Leave me alone, and I will go somewhere to hide behind the hills. Maybe then I can begin to understand. And on the way I will write slogans on the walls.—Fawaz Turki."

Another one for my collection.

"His?" I said, pointing to the top bunk.

"Yeah."

The tall one took it from me and carefully stuck it back in its place on the wall and smoothed it out.

"What's the charge against him?"

"I don't know. He been in this cell with us two weeks and ain't said nothin' to nobody. Look at this, man."

He reached under the foot of the mattress and handed me a thin, boxlike object.

"See here? It's a picture frame, man. The picture goes in here."

Hundreds of empty Pall Mall cigarette packages had been painstakingly folded and interlocked into a sturdy, well-made picture frame. You couldn't tell they were cigarette packages unless you looked closely. There was no picture in the frame.

"Turn it over."

I turned it over. The back was in the design of an American flag.

"Who made it?" I said.

"The guy here before him." Nodding at the top bunk. "He had all kinds of things, man."

Mouseman took it from the black and looked at it.

"What do you think?" I said, trying to get him to talk.

"That's nice, man. That's really nice."

"How are your mice?"

"They're okay, but I got too many of 'em now. I got to thin 'em out. You know anything about mice?"

"Not much."

I wanted a closer look at him.

"Can I see them again? Sit over here and show them to me."

He stood up and the two blacks moved over so he could

sit by the bars. He pulled the box from under the bunk and put it on his knees. Allowing for some mental and physical retardation he might have been fifteen. Or sixteen. But no way was he twenty-one, old enough to be in the Tombs. He should have been in the juvenile detention home on Rikers Island.

"How old are you?" I said.

"Twenty-one."

The two blacks were watching him. I had the impression they had wondered about his age too, but had not bothered to ask.

"I guess a lot of people must have asked you your age when you got busted," I said.

"Yeah." He lifted the top off the box.

"What did they bust you for?"

"I killed some guy."

"Did the cops believe you when you said you were twenty-one?"

"My mother showed them some school papers."

"I guess your lawyer asked, too, right? And the judge?"

"Yeah."

"Well, you know, like I said, I'm just a Legal Aid lawyer. I'm not a guard or an inmate or a cop or a judge or anything like that. You know that?"

"Yeah." He had his hand in the box, scooping up mice and letting them fall back through his fingers.

"So tell me, how old are you?"

"I'm twenty-one."

An idea hit me. "Have you ever been on Rikers Island?"

"Yeah, I was there once."

"How'd you like it?"

He shrugged. "It was okay."

"Okay?"

"Too many queens."

"How do you mean?"

"They used to dress up all the time. You have uniforms there. Not like here. They'd wash their shirts in mashed potatoes, put mashed potatoes in the water, and press them up against the walls and let them dry like that and they'd be like they'd been ironed, you know? And they'd cut down their pants and make them tight and then put red stuff on their faces they got off the bricks, and go around like girls." He hesitated. "I didn't like that."

"Did you ever have any trouble?"

He scooped up a handful of mice. "Anybody touched me, I'd kill him."

So he'd been raped a few times on Rikers and figured the Tombs was better than that. Not that he couldn't be raped in the Tombs, but it wasn't quite the wholesale kind of thing it was on Rikers.

"I've got to tell you, son. You're the first person I ever heard of who lied about his age to get into the Tombs."

He grinned, a bit too coyly.

"What's your name?" I asked.

The Afro answered. "Mouseman. They call him Mouseman."

"No. My name's Skinny."

"Well, Skinny, where'd you get all those mice?"

"I caught them the first night here, nine of them. That was all I caught. I've got to thin them out. You can't drown them. Their lungs fill up with water and they breathe it."

He plucked a dead mouse from the box and flipped it out through the bars. It landed somewhere in the darkness with a soft splash.

A paper cup partly torn at the top sat on a foot-square steel table welded to the cell wall. Skinny poured a few drops of coffee from the cup to the tabletop. Then he lifted ten or fifteen mice out of the box and put them on the table and watched them lick the coffee.

"He eats them," the Afro said, laughing.

"I do not."

"He cooks them and eats them."

I had already heard about the sophisticated culinary habits of some resourceful inmates. They burned tightly folded magazine pages under the steel tables and fried leftover food in butter saved from the regular meals. I didn't like to think of mice sizzling away on that make-shift grill.

"I do not," Skinny said.

"Ol' Geek ate one, though," the Afro said.

"I'll get him on the outside."

"They say you gonna get an education in jail," the Afro said. "Man, when Skinny get out, he gonna get hisself a job in a butcher shop."

The blacks laughed. Skinny took a halfhearted swing at the Afro and missed. They all laughed.

"How long you been in here?" I said to Skinny.

"Sixteen months."

"What've they offered you?"

"Two years."

"That sounds like a good offer. Maybe you should have taken it."

"I ain't coppin' out to no felony."

"Well they can't give you a misdemeanor for homicide."

"You cop out to a felony, you lose your car. I told my lawyer and the judge. I told 'em I wouldn't take no felony. I ain't gonna lose my car."

I said good night to them and moved up the section. I walked along slowly from cell to cell, talking quietly to anyone who wanted to talk. Most of them were the same crippled misfits who'd cluttered my office for seventeen years. One thing they all had in common: immediate living. No reasonable thought of past or future, no awareness of the life-trick by which deferment of pleasure enlarges it. Instead of dreams, they had demands. You saw them in amusement arcades. Coin in the slot, fire the missiles, sink the submarines, win or lose, instant joy or depression, put another coin in the slot. If you asked one where he was going, he said, "To hell." Ask him where he'd come from, and he gave you the name of his home town. He had a curse for the life-after, and like the rest of us no name at all for the life-before. They made me think of my own betrayals.

After a while I sat down alone on the flat's damp floor and leaned my back against the bars of a cell. The shapes inside were dark and silent. A sorrow for these men, for their victims, for myself, for the things we do and the things done to us, rose inside me stronger than the nausea. I put my head on my knees and tried to let it all out. But no tears came.

After several minutes I lifted my head and looked across the tables to the catwalk and the row of windows along the top of the wall. Mice ran on the table edges. If

I stared too long at the catwalk bars, they jumped toward me and away. On the other side of that wall was the island of Manhattan. I hoped I would be out there soon. I hoped we would all be out there soon.

I remembered when I was eight and my family had a duplex in a Fifth Avenue apartment house across from the Central Park Zoo. I lay awake at night, and in the pockets of silence between passing buses and taxis and sirens, I could hear the lions roar. I listened to the lions the way people in Harlem listen to cats fighting. I began to think that maybe I could sneak out of the apartment, ride down in the elevator, cross the street, and spend the night with the lions. Actually get in the cages with them and sleep there. I thought about it, and then I told my friends that I had done it. They were greatly impressed. I often repeated the claim, and still do sometimes. In my teens, it impressed girls. And as an attorney, it's been a playful test of the gullibility of associates. Susan believed it, or said she did.

After an hour sitting on the floor looking across at the bars, I stood up and started back to the bridge. I stopped at one cell where a man was leaning against the bars with his forearms in bandages. We began to talk and he told me that three days earlier he had rented a fragment of broken razor blade from an inmate on the flat.

"I gave him seventeen cigarettes," he said in the darkness, "and six slices of bread and a bar of soap. He said it was cheap, I'd get a trip out to Bellevue. I told him I didn't want no trip to nowhere but the morgue. He said, fine, then you won't need none of them things you got. So I gave him my stuff. He gave me the blade and he watched me with it. Then he took it back and when I was bleedin' he called The Man on me, and they did this." He thrust his arms angrily through the bars. "And now I ain't got nothin'."

He stared at the bandages. "I paid but I didn't get. You pay for everything in here. You pay to die. But they don't deliver."

I try to learn things from my guards, what's going on outside, but they won't speak. They talk to the other inmates. I don't care. The youngest one—long hair, skinny—walked slowly by my cell this morning. He stopped for a second and looked in. I was naked, sitting on the edge of the bunk. He had something he wanted to say. Encouragement? A warning? His lips parted, but before he could speak, a guard at the end of the corridor yelled, "Kirk!" and he hurried away. It doesn't matter. The loneliness and the hate I've had before. A man with a strong ego can't be hurt with hate. He eats hate. What bothers me is a steady draining away of confidence. I'm not sure now that justice even exists, or is desirable. "There is a point beyond which even justice becomes unjust." That's Sophocles. Pursuing justice is like pursuing the perfect woman. True justice, true love. Myths. I don't really believe that. Do I? It had to be done. Someone had to do it.

I thought about the young guard, Kirk. Or maybe it was Kurk—first name, last name, I wasn't sure. I stood up, paced for a moment, and lay down on the floor. The tile was cool under my back. The older guard, the one who had yelled at Kirk, walked by, eyes front, not even a glance for this naked lunatic sprawled on the floor. An inmate up the row began to howl—long, gentle, birdlike cries of boredom or madness. *Ohhhhhhhhhhhhhhhhh!!! Whooooooooooooooooooo!!!* I joined him, crying softly at first, then louder, much louder, screaming. In a few seconds I was yelling for all I was worth, throwing such a fit as I would not have dared even in childhood. Prison admits many liberties enjoined on the outside.

I exhausted myself with howls and screams and then lay still on the tiles, chest heaving. Everything was quiet. No guard had made a move to silence me. There are no eccentrics here. Insanity is taken for granted, and we are free to indulge its delicious symptoms.

SEVEN

T HE NEXT afternoon I was back on the street—in the sunshine, on the pavement, breathing in the sweet exhaust of some so-silent bus. Unable to insert more prisoners into the city's rioting jails, the courts had been forced to parole everyone arrested during the night. I told the warden on the phone that morning that if they were releasing new prisoners immediately at their arraignment, they should think about paroling some of the old ones already in jail. He said some people wanted to talk to me about that, and what effect it would have on the rioters. He said the previous night's TV broadcast had had a powerful impact.

I told Oscar I thought it was time to move my negotiating out of the jail.

He agreed. I was not unhappy that he did.

A hundred reporters, photographers and television people mobbed me on the sidewalk when I came out of the Tombs. I spotted Fischer at the curb with one of the DA's cars and pushed toward him.

Men jammed microphones in my face, and one of them said, "Since you're the one who seems to have started this problem, Mr. Dori, can you give us any answers?"

I had had no intention of saying anything, but that

question made me angry. These guys always know so fucking much.

"I don't think it's a time for answers," I said.

That stopped him.

"If a building's burning down, the first thing is to get the people out. You don't go around asking for answers to the problems of fireproofing."

"Then how *do* we get the people out?" he said.

"Unlock the doors."

By that time I was in Fischer's car, pulling away. Susan was in the back seat. She leaned over and kissed me. I reached back to hold her hand, and faced Fischer.

He made a face. "Dori, I hate to be the first to tell you, but you really smell like shit."

"David," I said, "that is *exactly* what I smell like."

We turned left and headed uptown.

"I'm supposed to take you to Rhein's chambers," Fischer said. "He wants a little chat with you, not surprisingly. But maybe you ought to go home and clean up first. I'll wait for you."

"Hell, no. Let's go right to Rhein's. It appeals to me, taking a whiff of the Tombs into the heart of the exalted episcopate. It might do them good. What's been happening?"

Susan answered. "They've been paroling everyone brought to court since yesterday noon, all new prisoners."

"You were on television last night," Fischer said. "That was some scene, Al. Unbelievable."

Susan said, "Simon heard the Mayor's office had more phone calls after that show than ever before about anything."

"I think they've got quite a collection waiting for you at Rhein's," Fischer said.

"What do you mean?"

"The DA's going, I know, so I would imagine you'll find a few others, too."

"Now they want to talk," I said.

"There's been some violence, too," Susan said.

I had the feeling Fischer had hoped she wouldn't mention it.

"What violence?"

Fischer answered. "A little fire and trashing in Harlem last night. Some kids tore up a few shops on 125th Street. There aren't enough cops."

I had never been in Rhein's chambers before, but nothing there surprised me. The room was vast, thickly carpeted, dark-paneled. Small men need big offices.

Rhein was alone, lost behind a huge kidney-shaped desk. I had seen one of those desks in the Brooklyn DA's office. Inmates make them in state prisons. I'm sure it satisfied Rhein enormously to work every day on an artifact produced by the consumers of his justice.

"Sit down, Mr. Dori."

His tiny, wizened old head rose like a white lump behind the desk. He indicated a chair twenty feet from the desk. We would have to shout at each other.

"I've invited the DA and the Police Commissioner and the Correction Commissioner and one or two others. We can talk while we wait for them, but I'd like to stay away from the substantive matters until they get here."

He then proceeded to jump right into the "substantive matters."

"You've been in jail, I believe, the past few hours, so perhaps you are unaware of what is going on."

I thought it necessary to establish myself immediately. I did not want him to think that I had come to be talked at and impressed.

"I think my being in jail has had the opposite effect," I said.

The lump elevated one or two inches.

"Dori, let us understand one thing at the start. I know all about you. I do not intend to tolerate your sarcasm. You may consider this a joking matter, but I assure you the Appellate Division does not."

"Then while we are understanding each other," I said, "and establishing ground rules, let me contribute something. I have come here directly from the Tombs. I have not slept. I have spent the past twenty-four hours immersed in excrement, listening to the tales of the damned. I am totally and if need be violently on the side of the defendants, as you are not. I regard it as highly significant that this is the first time I, or to my knowledge any working attorney of the Legal Aid Society, has been in this room on any but the most formal occasions. Never before have you sought contact with any of us, or information from any of us. Never have you asked our opinions on how justice might be increased for the accused. Your only concern has been to clear calendars, to get the defendants as swiftly as possible out of your judicial hair. You have shown great concern for machinery and none whatsoever for individuals, neither the accused nor the complainants. I have just survived the filth and violence of twenty-four hours in the Tombs, and I expect to survive without difficulty some few minutes in your antiseptic chambers. So let's not try to cow each other."

His face was red. He was an old man, and I thought perhaps I had gone too far.

"Since it appears to be a time for bluntness, Mr. Dori, I will be blunt." He stood up, trembling with emotion. "You have threatened the entire criminal justice system of this state. Irresponsibly, as some kind of a practical joke perhaps, you have brought violence to the courts, to the city jails, and to the streets. Perhaps you have not heard that six people died last night in Harlem riots. Four children were killed in an apartment fire because firemen were striking. In Bedford-Stuyvesant, armed thugs wandered the streets last night, robbing at will. We have virtually no policemen on the street. And now we are being forced to turn those people arrested last night back into the streets. Are you proud, Mr. Dori? Is this what you call increasing justice? Well, you are not going to get away with it."

He had taken me by surprise. Fischer and Susan should have told me.

"I can think of nothing I want to get away with, your honor. On the contrary, I am trying to stop a general 'getting-away-with' that's gotten rather out of hand. I am distressed that those people died, and that perhaps more will die, but I am frankly more concerned with the preservation of justice than with the preservation of a few random lives."

"You are a heartless son of a bitch, Mr. Dori."

That got to me.

"Don't you talk to me like that! You're worried about

six people who died in Harlem. When were you in court last? When were you in the Tombs last? Six people. How many times that number die each year in the Tombs and all the hell holes like it? I've stood around like an acquiescent robot for seventeen years and watched more violence than comes to Harlem in many, many nights. I will stand around no longer. All you hear is your own voice echoing off these beautiful dark walls—"

"Dori, if you think you can highjack the judicial system, if you think—"

I rose and started for the door. I was afraid of doing something really foolish. I was afraid he was about to have a coronary.

At the door, I took a deep breath and tried to calm myself. I wanted to leave with some dignity.

"Have you ever heard of Stanislaus Lec?" I asked.

He stood there glaring at me, speechless.

"He described men like you. He said, 'The dispensing of injustice is always in the right hands.'"

He leaned his tiny, frail body on the top of that mammoth desk and rasped at me. "You won't get away with this. I don't care how crazy you are or how brilliant you are, or whatever you want to call yourself. I don't care if you've got every young radical in Legal Aid and the DA's office, and all the inmates in every jail in the city. I'm going to stop you, and I'm going to do it, if I have to, all alone, with my bare hands."

His hands were white, fragile, bony. He held them out, palms up, exactly as Dunlop had held out his.

I opened the door and walked out. The secretary was standing there, mouth open.

"I think he needs a pill," I said.

Fischer and Susan were waiting for me in the car.

"What happened?" Fischer said, starting the engine.

"Nothing."

"Who was there?" Susan asked.

"Nobody."

We rode in silence back to the apartment.

"I'm sorry," I said to Fischer, getting out of the car. "I'm too tired to talk. I lost my temper and blew up at him. He's such an old fart. I'll call you later. Can we have dinner or something and talk about it?"

"Call me whenever you're ready."

When we got up to my floor I said to Susan, "Have you got your key?" She'd said she was moving in.

She didn't answer, just looked a little nervous, like was I now going to blow up at her.

"So you didn't move in."

She let her silence answer.

I kept my mouth shut. Anything I said would be something I'd be sorry for.

I took a shower and put on a bathrobe. She was waiting for me on the sofa with a drink. I sat down and leaned my head back. I felt much better, clean and relaxed. I was home. I was safe. Nothing bad could happen to me here.

"I really blew it with Rhein. I don't even have any idea what he wanted to see me about. I know he didn't get me over there just to insult me. What the hell am I going to do now?"

"Why don't you take a nap?"

"Why do I hate him so much? What the hell can he do?

175

He's a stupid, heartless, complacent bastard, but what the hell could he do anyway? What the hell can anyone do?"

She relaxed back against the cushions and put her head on my shoulder.

"Maybe there's something I don't know. I keep assuming the public would improve the courts and the jails if they really understood how killing they are. But maybe what we've got is just exactly the criminal justice setup everyone really wants. Compared to most other countries it's a dream. Other places they don't even have habeas corpus."

I let out a deep sigh and closed my eyes. I was falling asleep.

"It's very frustrating not having a clearly identified hate object. What we need are more villains."

"Why don't you take a nap?"

I looked at my watch. It was four o'clock. "Come to bed with me. At six I'll make some calls."

Half an hour later, the phone rang. I had to answer it. This was not my day.

"Mr. Dori, this is Robert Patterson at the Appellate Division. We've met, but I'm not sure if you—"

"Oh, yes. Sure I do."

He was a legal assistant to Rhein. The couple of times I'd met him he'd seemed like a nice guy—young, bright, maybe a little too correct. Not loose enough. Working for Rhein could do that.

"Justice Rhein suggested that if you still wish to participate in the meeting with the District Attorney and the Commissioners of Police and Correction, you might all get together this evening. He regrets that he has a dinner at

Gracie Mansion and won't be able to attend, but he will have a representative present."

I had to laugh.

"Mr. Patterson, you have a very tough job. I mean working for that bastard. To begin with, it was not as a result of my wishes that my participation was sought. And secondly, it is truly pathetic, though not at all surprising, that his lordship regards dinner with the Mayor as more important than the preservation of justice. That's if he really *is* going to Gracie Mansion, and isn't just too chicken to—"

Susan dug her nails into my arm.

"I'm sorry, Patterson. Maybe the PJ told you I'm a little touchy right now."

"I understand completely, Mr. Dori. What shall I tell Justice Rhein?"

"Tell him that I will miss his presence enormously, but will attend nevertheless. Where?"

"In his chambers."

"He got the place bugged or something?"

"At seven? Is that too early?"

"Seven's fine. Thanks very much."

I hung up and Susan said, "You'd better get some sleep before you go. If you don't want to end up getting arrested."

Rhein's representative at the meeting turned out to be Patterson himself. He had plates of sandwiches set out, and Cokes. The DA and Correction Commissioner were warm enough, but the PC looked at me like I was something pulled up out of the sewer. He was a tall, thin, red-haired man named William Karp. He got things going very quickly, as if he didn't want to be in the same room with me any longer than necessary.

"The situation is this," he said, referring to papers he took from an attaché case. "As of one hour ago, our Bureau of Operations had recorded for the past twenty-four hours one hundred and twenty-seven instances of unopposed street robberies—muggings, that is—that we feel can be directly related to the absence of police officers who would normally have been on post or patrol in the immediate vicinity. Slightly more than two-thirds involved groups of more than two perpetrators. Nearly one-third occurred in so-called low-frequency crime areas, that is, the seventeenth and nineteenth precincts on Manhattan's East Side, Brooklyn Heights, and similar areas. Nine of these robberies ended as homicides."

He put the papers down, leaned back in his chair, and looked solemnly out at us from under bushy red eyebrows. "The most serious thing about these figures is that when you consider the number of groups and the insurgence into previously unabused areas, relatively unabused areas, you are forced to conclude that the almost total absence of enforcement is producing an atmosphere of freedom and willfulness. Those who have gone into the streets and robbed, or into stores and robbed, and encountered absolutely no resistance, can be expected to spread the word. These incursions into low-crime areas, for example, can be expected to increase rapidly once those perpetrators get back to their own neighborhoods and report their success. They have a situation now that must strike them as too good to be true, as some kind of Christmas."

"Do you have any figures on the rate of increase of these—" It was Steven Burk, the DA—young, levelheaded, very low tolerance for bullshit.

"No. Not yet. But we're working up some charts. They'll be ready in the morning. By then we'll have more information."

"How limited is your enforcement? Have you any men coming in now at all?" Still Burk.

"Virtually none. We've managed to keep a few undercovers in the field, and their help will be valuable in assessing moods and anticipating trends. They tend as a group to be more committed than the average officer, and they're less interested in police politics, unions, that sort of thing. But aside from them, we are almost completely without men."

He picked up another paper. "As of the morning tour today, the percentages of men reporting were as follows: Patrolmen, .13 percent. Sergeants, .70 percent. Lieutenants and above, 52 percent. Detectives, 18 percent. Most of the men who did report, including ranking officers, are on the streets in sector cars. Even the borough commanders, Chief of Detectives, Chief Inspector, men like that, are out patrolling in sector cars."

"I'd like—" The Correction Commissioner started to speak. His name was Joe Osterman. He was the same age as Karp, mid-fifties, and they had grown up together in that slice of West Side Manhattan that used to be called Hell's Kitchen. He was short but thick, and tough.

"Excuse me," Karp said, cutting him off, "just one thing more. And this relates to the Tombs and other houses of detention. The figures I just read to you, for the number

179

of robberies, these all occurred, we believe, as a result of reduction in available officers. The effect of paroling of jailed defendants is yet to be determined."

"I was just going to mention," Osterman said, "that before I came over here I received some very disturbing reports from inmate informants. Including—" he nodded at Karp, the PC—"an unexpected communication from one of your men I didn't even know was in the house."

Everyone chuckled.

"The reports all said that once word got around about the paroling of jail inmates, the spirit in the detention houses was one of hysterical elation. I brought some of these reports with me."

He reached thick stubby fingers into a manila envelope and came up with a sheaf of blue papers.

"From an inmate in the Brooklyn House of Detention for Men—" His eyes skimmed down the page. "My cellmates and the men on the flat were talking about what they were gonna do first when they got out, who they was gonna kill first, what they was gonna rob first. They said now you can do anything you wanted because there was no pigs left and if you walked into court and surrendered they wouldn't take you."

He read another one from the Tombs, and another from the Queens House of Detention for Men. I had stopped listening. This was the first I'd heard they'd started paroling men out of the jails. I wanted to stand up and cheer. I struggled to keep from laughing.

"When did you start paroling men from the jails?" I asked.

"At four this afternoon," Patterson said. "About fifty men from each jail, low-bail cases."

"And how long do you expect to continue?"

"Until conditions are relieved and we regain some flexibility. I would say a couple or three days maybe."

"Until a 'controllable normality' is regained," Burk said with a touch of sarcasm. "I don't know what that means. I'm not sure it means anything. But I think that was the phrase Justice Rhein used, was it not?" He didn't like paroling prisoners.

"Yes, sir," Patterson said. "I believe that was the phrase."

"That's why we had hoped you would come here and talk to us," Burk said to me. He was the only one in the room with a tie on. I wished he'd at least unbutton the collar. It made me hotter just looking at him.

"I had been wondering why," I said.

Patterson said, "Justice Rhein had wanted to be here himself to ask you to go back."

"Back into the Tombs?" He had to be kidding. This Rhein was unbelievable.

"Yes, sir," Patterson said.

"He's got to be out of his fucking mind. Why doesn't he go into the Tombs himself?"

"The problem is this, Allan," Burk said. "We're going along with this paroling thing because obviously it got to the point where something had to be done to relieve conditions in the jails. You were very impressive on television last night. I don't think many people realized how hellish it was in there until they saw that film. You had a lot of balls going in, and staying in, and no one would ask you to go back without very good reasons. But as I say, although we're going along with the paroling, we're afraid —at least I'm very afraid—that it could get out of hand.

When the inmates see men leaving, they're all going to want to go. And we cannot, absolutely cannot, afford to parole any of the heavy cases. The effect on enforcement would be disastrous. So while the paroling will relieve physical conditions somewhat, it will also increase tension, psychological tension so to speak. Do you follow me?"

"Absolutely."

"Now, we have reliable information, and you no doubt know this yourself, that the men in the Tombs are controlled to a great extent by certain leaders. We think we've identified them, and as a matter of fact we have rather extensive files on them."

He rested his hand on a brown attaché case by his chair.

"We'll go over them with you if you like. We are hoping you will consent to return to the Tombs, contact these men, determine their stand, and if possible try to reason with them. The inmates showed yesterday and last night and this morning that they trust you. You can talk to them reasonably, and they'll listen. They have to be reasonably but firmly prepared for the fact that this paroling is strictly limited and will not under any circumstances extend to other than low-bail cases."

"What do you call low bail?"

"Up to twenty-five hundred."

The figure was not arbitrary. It's the amount above which most bail jumping occurs.

Burk stopped talking, and the four men stared at me. Except for Patterson, they were New York street men. They were brought up in the streets, put themselves through local schools, fought to get where they were.

They couldn't think of many reasons for liking a Legal Aid attorney—especially not a rich one, and *especially* not one who had, as they saw it, started this whole mess.

"Will you do it?" Burk asked finally.

"No."

Karp's jaws tensed.

"You see, gentlemen," I said, "there's something you don't understand. I'm on their side."

"How *can* you be?" Karp exploded, as if I'd just said I was in love with a German shepherd.

Burk threw him a quick, conciliating look. "No, it's easy to understand. It's completely proper, of course, and we don't take any exception to it, Allan. But what we're asking you to do will help them."

He wasn't even perspiring.

"Help them," I said, "but not help *them*. I didn't mean I was on the side of the few specific defendants rioting in the jails. I'm on the side of *all* the defendants who will ever be. That puts me on the side of the rioters who want to destroy the jails and the police and the courts and even the DA's office. I and they want to destroy those things for very different reasons, I'm sure, but we both want to destroy them. I want to do it so someone will have to build a modern judicial structure that will work—and that will be built on *exactly* the same basic principles as the present one."

"He's crazy," Karp said under his breath, just loud enough for me to hear.

"So my motives are totally different from those of the men in your files there. Those men are criminals and anarchists and revolutionaries. I am just one of your old-fashioned reactionaries who wants everything to work the way it worked fifty years ago."

Burk nodded—sagely, sadly, a fine judicial aspect on his brow. Someday he'd be a beautiful judge.

"What if we paroled a few men, and then stopped and there were more riots? Would you go back then?"

"No."

"Fuck him," Karp said, gathering his papers. "He told us where he stands. He's on their side. So why are we talking to him? I'm getting out of here."

The meeting broke up, and I went home.

At eleven o'clock that night Susan and I watched a special on WCBS-TV called, "Is Justice Dead?" It went on for two hours—cops and emergency equipment outside the rioting jails, cops at station houses who reported for duty, cops at home who didn't report, blacks rampaging in Harlem, the fire that killed the four children, interviews with the Mayor, the Police Commissioner, the Correction Commissioner. Interviews and interviews. They had even tried to talk to me. Susan said they called the office for me while I was in the Tombs and had called the apartment while I was sleeping. She told them I was out. They didn't miss anyone else. They even interviewed a Mafia boss, who sounded as appalled by the violence as everyone else, followed by some network pundit commenting wryly that, after all, the city was now threatened not by organized crime, which could be reasoned with and bribed, but by disorganized crime, whose violence was mindless as an earthquake.

Susan and I sat there on the sofa eating sandwiches and drinking beer. Not infrequently a speaker mentioned me by name, never to my advantage. Some said I was a publicity-seeking opportunist getting ready to run for office. Some implied I was part of a meticulously organized, nationwide conspiracy of revolutionaries. One charitable cop said I was just nuts.

Susan played cheerleader for the underdog, defending me to the TV with cries of, "Idiot! Fool!" But when they showed the Harlem rioting, the stores and tenements burning, firemen sliding stretchers with children on them into ambulances, she was silent.

I wondered if Bianchi was watching, and whose side he was on. I remembered that man's ripped earlobe on the sidewalk in front of the court building. Why was I doing this? Was I *sure*? What is the morally acceptable price of justice when the currency is blood? What if I was wrong?

"What if I was wrong?"

Fire trucks poured water into a burning store.

"It's too late now," she said.

Was there accusation in her tone, just a tiny ripple she could not suppress?

Blacks threw bricks at firemen. The camera cut to firemen scuffling with blacks. Then to the ambulances.

Neither of us spoke. A cloud of nervous embarrassment, heavy as the TV smoke, came down around us. I tried to think of something to say. It was like a first date. Someone *had* to say something.

The Fire Commissioner, interviewed on the scene in Harlem, said how handicapped they were by a shortage of men.

I got up and walked into the bedroom and lay down. I needed someone on my side, someone who was absolutely *certain*. I closed my eyes. The TV went off. I didn't hear her footsteps, but I felt the bed tip. She touched my cheek.

"It doesn't matter, Allan. If there were a thousand more—"

This tough-as-nails revolutionary here. She disgusted me. I disgusted myself. I was incoherent with exhaustion.

"Why don't you go to sleep, Allan?"

It was more like passing out. I woke up in the dark under the covers with my clothes still on. Susan was next to me naked. I got up quietly and undressed. I got back in bed, and couldn't go to sleep. I kept thinking about the TV show. All those guys always know so fucking much. They had years and decades to fix this mess and now someone does something and they're all self-righteous experts. If you want to be hated, tell a complacent man where he's wrong. And if you want to be hated unto death, *show* him where he's wrong. They *were* wrong. I was right. All I had to do was remember Alicia Bonner, and the suicides, and Skinny the Mouseman, and hundreds and hundreds of others. I paraded them out like sheep, counting them one by one—a winding, endless, surrealistic death march of defendants.

"Allan."

Susan had her hand lightly on my chest.

"Allan."

"Yes."

"Are you all right?"

"What's wrong?"

"You were talking in your sleep. You were shouting."

"What did I say?"

"I couldn't understand. You sounded awful. I thought maybe you were sick. Are you all right?"

"I'm fine."

I looked at my watch. It was four A.M. I lay there and fell back half asleep. Then I was awake again, completely awake. Susan had withdrawn her hand and turned over and gone to sleep. I was suddenly frightened. I was terrified. I got quickly out of bed and stood straight and motionless in the dark. I felt panicked, a claustrophobe in a straitjacket. I wanted people and lights and noise. Immediately. All the reality I could get. I rushed into the living room and turned on lights. I switched on the TV and flipped through empty channels till I got a film. I turned it up loud. I turned on the FM. I opened a window and put my head out and watched automobile headlights moving up the avenue. I was standing like that when Susan put her arms around my waist. I left the window open and went over to the sofa. We sat there with the TV going and the radio going. After four or five minutes, Susan said, "Can I turn the radio and TV down?"

I nodded and she got up. She turned them off, and then switched off the lights. "Okay?"

"Okay."

She came back to the sofa, and we stretched out. I started telling her about the Tombs. She lay there still and quiet, and I told her everything. Every minute, every word. I told her about the meeting with Rhein and the meeting later with the whole group. She didn't make a sound.

"I hate what those men think of me, Susan. I was establishment, I was one of them. And now they look at me

187

like something dirty. Most of them are good men inside. They don't want to hurt anyone. I was like that myself for seventeen years. I don't like being hated by men like that. And the ones who are cheering me now, the inmates, the scum and the filth, I don't want to be cheered by them. The good men hate me, and the bad ones love me—both for the wrong reasons. If just one honest, knowing, intelligent man would say, 'Dori, you're right. I'm with you, man. All the way.' But no one does. Not one."

"Simon's on your side."

"Simon's a fool."

"Fischer?"

"Fischer's a black bourgeois opportunist. He's a politician. I like him, but let's face it, he wants to be the first black governor of New York. And what makes you so sure he's on my side?"

I stopped talking. The fear was gone. We lay there till the sun came up. Then I dozed off for a minute, and when I woke up Susan was in the kitchen. She heard me and yelled, "Hey, flip on the TV for a second, will you?"

I got up and pushed the button. Nothing happened. I checked the plug. Susan had cut it off.

"What'd you do that for?" I said.

She came into the living room with orange juice. "It's an evil machine, so I castrated it."

Now, you have to love a girl like that.

Nothing defines like absence. In the next week New Yorkers learned what law-and-order is. Because they had none. None at all. No cops, no firemen, no ambulances, no subway, no garbage collection, no mail. The city was on its own. The people were on their own. Striking cops and firemen rented themselves out as guards to banks, hotels, department stores, and office buildings. The downstairs lobby in my own apartment house had four men there day and night in civilian clothes, armed with baseball bats, pistols and shotguns. Some cops formed what they, and television newcasters, called "law squads." They drove through the city in cars and trucks, battling muggers and looters, often with automatic weapons on both sides.

Susan moved in with me, and the first night she had a remarkably calm but terrifying call from her brother. His name was Dick—the engineer, the one who watched her take a shot at her father. He lived with his wife and two children in an unguarded apartment house on Central Park West. At nine P.M. they were watching television when they heard people moving around and talking in the hall.

"At first I thought it was someone's party guests," he told Susan on the phone, "but when the noise didn't stop I went to the door to see what the trouble was."

He cracked his door and saw four black men with drawn pistols. He slammed the door, locked it with all four locks, and dialed 911, the police emergency number. Naturally it didn't answer. He heard the men banging on apartment doors. They banged on his. He got his pistol from over the ventilator in the kitchen and sent his wife and children into the bedroom. Then he set a small table across the living room from the door, put the phone on the table off the hook, still ringing the 911 number, and sat down behind the table with the gun steady in both hands, aiming at the door.

"I could hear them knocking around in the hall and I could hear the phone ringing. I was hoping the cops would answer, but I knew they wouldn't. If those bastards came through the door I was going to empty the gun into them."

He sat there for an hour. They did not break through the door. They broke through someone else's door. He heard the pounding and crashing and screams and gunshots.

"They were out there for an hour," he said, "just taking their time about it."

When they left he called us. He said his wife was hysterical, and the children were so terrified they couldn't speak. He wanted to get out of the city—in my car.

"Martha's family have a house outside Newark," he said. "I hate to ask, but we can't stay here, and none of the neighbors . . . It shouldn't take more than an hour."

What could I do? I told him I'd drive them, but not at night, they'd have to wait till morning, and he'd have to hold his wife, Martha, on his lap and jam the children in back. All I had was a Porsche. It wasn't designed for refugees.

I left at 6 A.M. Four guards were on duty in the lobby.

"How's it going?" I said to one of them.

"No problems. Nothing to worry about at all. Safe and sound."

The reassurance was that of a father to a frightened child. He was short, heavy, about twenty-five, and wore a black patrolman's belt with revolver and handcuffs. He was in shirtsleeves, sitting on a wooden chair in the doorway. The other guards called him Sammy. We talked for a moment, but he made no move to get out of the door-way. Not from rudeness—it just didn't occur to him that I might want to venture beyond the scope of his protection.

"Excuse me," I said, moving toward the door.

"He stood up and dragged the chair aside. "Careful out there," he said. "I wouldn't advise going out there."

I looked out and saw nothing but a deserted street, buildings, and a few parched trees. "Just going down the block to the garage," I said.

He nodded dubiously.

Martha sat on Dick's lap and didn't say a word. The children—both girls, seven and nine—behaved as if their slightest word or movement would detonate the universe. None of them had slept.

Dick was embarrassed, determined to make sure I realized how bad things were. "They went through the whole building," he said. "Eight floors. They killed two people, raped—"

Martha turned swollen red eyes on him.

"No one could get the police, or an ambulance, or—"

"*Please*," Martha said, and he stopped talking and pressed her head against his shoulder. The girls didn't move.

The house was on the western fringes of Newark, and Dick was right that the trip shouldn't have taken more than an hour. In fact, it took four hours. Every car in New York was bumper-to-bumper between the West Side Highway and a quarter-mile of the house. As if on some intuitive biological signal, New Yorkers had suddenly rushed for the exits.

Toll booths on the George Washington Bridge were abandoned, their windows smashed. The bridge itself took forty-five minutes. We crept along behind a red Dodge filled with half a neighborhood. A dog and a small boy were squashed against the rear window. The boy gazed back at us. I waved, but he made no sign.

Beyond the bridge we passed stalled cars pulled onto the shoulder, hoods up, radiators gushing steam. A young man in long hair and a yellow T-shirt was next to a Volvo with two girls in it. He wanted a ride. No one had room. He came toward us and Dick rolled his window closed. The boy looked in and knocked on the window and shouted. "Just the girls! Just the girls!" He had a moustache.

"No room!" Dick shouted. And then to me, "Dumb bastard. How's he think we're gonna get two more people in here? Let him in and he'll grab the car."

The man left us and went on to the cars behind. He looked desperate. The heat was stifling. I left my window open, but kept an eye on the rear view mirror.

I dropped them off at the house and started back. I was the only one headed into Manhattan. People standing around stalled cars waved madly at me. They didn't care which way I was going. I remembered Dick's words. They just wanted the car. Four people, two of them women, ran into the road ahead of me. They waved, and when I slowed down they joined hands across the road. I thought of myself trying to walk the miles back to the apartment. I thought of Susan there alone. I stepped on the gas, flipped on the lights, and pressed the horn. I was on top of them, not fifty feet away, before they dropped their arms and scattered.

I stuck with the West Side Highway down to the 80s, then turned off and took Riverside Drive. At 74th Street five men were boosting themselves into the first-floor window of a brownstone. As I slowed down a wooden chair came crashing through a window above them, followed by picture frames and pillows. On the fourth floor a woman leaned out watching. She bent over the sill to look down at the men coming in, and the furniture flying out, and then straightened up and searched frantically through the air around her, left and right, up and down, as if the building were on fire and she hoped for a hook and ladder to pluck her to safety. She disappeared from the window and returned with an old man. They looked down at my car. Then the man disappeared and the woman continued her search for rescue.

They were as much beyond my aid as the people on the highway. The only person I felt responsible for now was Susan. Barriers were coming up between me and the apartment.

I cut over to Broadway and turned right. All the stores were closed. The farther downtown I went the more smashed windows I saw, and the more people there were on the street. Most of the people were black or Puerto Rican. Harlem had come downtown.

Lincoln Center was littered with broken glass. At Columbus Circle I got a look down toward Times Square and saw mobs and smoke. I slowed down and turned left into 58th Street. People were crawling on hands and knees in and out of a drugstore's smashed display window. A man lay face down on the sidewalk. A woman of about fifty stopped and looked at him, then bent over and grabbed his sleeve and tugged. He didn't move. She tugged again. He didn't move. She let go and stepped back and looked at him. Then she turned and walked off.

I drove back to the apartment with the windows closed and doors locked.

I told Susan what had happened and took a shower. We talked about trying to get out of the city. I decided against it. After all, our building was guarded. We sat at the window and watched traffic on First Avenue and the East River Drive. It was as bad as the West Side. Drivers wandered among stalled cars and wrecks, examining damage, arguing, peering ahead to discern some end to the chaos. No end was in sight, even to us from our high perch. A roar, distant but sustained, rose like the cry of a caged animal from the hopeless tangle of honking cars.

It was then, looking southwest at the traffic, that we first noticed a thin column of black smoke rising from what I guessed was the Bedford-Stuyvesant section of Brooklyn. For the rest of the day, and for the remainder of our time in the apartment, the base of the column broadened.

When I got up the next morning the first thing I noticed was the absence of the roar of honking cars. It was over. First Avenue and the Drive were littered with abandoned cars, but the occupants were gone. A lone car could make it now, weaving through the wreckage. I had no idea where all the people were—if they had escaped the city by doubling up in surviving cars, or if they had walked out, or gone back home. The desperate exodus had been like some curious natural phenomenon that suddenly appears, then vanishes.

Newspapers were still being published, but not delivered. The deliverers' union had ordered its drivers not to risk taking them through the streets. The *Times* said anyone who wanted a paper could have it for free by going to the loading platforms on West 43rd Street in Times Square. I imagine they had few takers.

I spliced the TV plug back on its cord.

The television stations, themselves heavily guarded by strikers, suspended regular programming and presented a round-the-clock horror show of a war zone that used to be New York City.

I have to admit that the television coverage was superb. It was a war, and they covered it as a war. Television crews went into the streets and with great bravery filmed the looting, arson and assaults. Often the crews themselves were attacked. Cameramen filmed attacks on sound men, sound men recorded attacks on cameramen.

Never before had the TV people had a war so logistically simple to cover, a war that allowed them to show what they could really do when they were given all the equipment, facilities and personnel available in New York. They did everything. They even went at it as a sporting event, complete with slow motion and instant replays. And why not? The networks displayed enormous courage, dazzling competence, limitless resourcefulness. And they loved every minute of it.

They gave the war balance. While some crews were in the streets filming violence and carnage, others were at City Hall, the Criminal Courts Building, Police Headquarters, interviewing city officials. You have never seen and heard such stunning portraits of confusion, pettiness and dissension. The Sanitation Commissioner demanded guards for his men so they could resume performance of the city's most needed service, the collection of garbage. The Transit Authority demanded guards for its men because transportation was the city's most vital service. Mail deliverers demanded . . . And so on. Meanwhile, the war continued—all of it strung out for posterity on endless reels of placidly revolving Scotch video tape.

In the Tombs and other city jails, the rioting continued off and on. The authorities had paroled some inmates the day of my meeting with Rhein, purely as a means of appeasing rioters. Officials negotiated through the night with Butterfield and other riot leaders and thought they made some headway. But when no more prisoners were called out for parole the next morning, the rioters stopped talking and went back to threats and violence. Oscar and other leaders in the Tombs threatened to storm the first floor and break into the street. In Brooklyn, a guard was badly beaten, then released. By afternoon the paroling had resumed in all boroughs, still low-bail cases.

The following afternoon, no more low-bail cases remained. The only prisoners still locked up were in the over-$2,500 class—robbers, murderers, rapists, heroin wholesalers. Paroling stopped.

Ever since that first street assault of a defendant who pleaded guilty, it had been clear that the prisoners had outside sympathy, perhaps even an organization. Now, with paroling halted, Warden Dunlop, the DA, and other officials started getting phone calls from men claiming to represent the prisoners. One said he was calling for "Prisoners' Liberation." Another that he spoke for the Black Liberation Army. A third, that he represented the Prisoners' Lib Black Liberation Army. They all had the same message. "Continue to release prisoners, and release them all, or greater violence will follow." They threatened bombings, arson, kidnappings, assassinations.

An hour after the second telephoned threat, Henry Trouman, public relations director for the Department of Correction, a man who had been often seen on television the past several days, was shot and killed coming out of his home in Yonkers. Five minutes after the shooting, a man called the National Broadcasting Company and said the "execution" had been performed by the Black Liberation Army.

The afternoon of the Trouman killing, Susan called me to the window overlooking Tudor City's small private park. About thirty or forty men, mostly black, were in the park tearing up benches and small trees. Three guards yelled at them from the door of the building next door. Two of the blacks with a piece of wood ripped from a bench ran up the block to a bookstore and knocked out the windows.

A small group of blacks, perhaps ten, then approached the guards, waving sticks and the iron endpiece of a bench. A fourth guard appeared in the door with a shotgun, and the men withdrew several steps.

A second group of blacks approached the door of my building, yelling at the guards I couldn't see in the doorway beneath the window.

"We comin' in, man," one of them called. "We gone come in an' crack your ass."

One black with a slat from a bench charged forward out of sight beneath me, then leaped back. I caught a glimpse of a swinging arm and a baseball bat. Three blacks jumped forward again into the door and this time ran back pursued by the police-belted guard, Sammy, swinging a bat. One of them grabbed the end of the bat. Two others leaped at Sammy, seized his arm, and dragged him struggling into the middle of the street. The group next door ran to join them. I heard an explosion and saw an orange blast from the next-door guard's shotgun. Two blacks fell in the street. Others ran for cover in the park. The three men with Sammy had him down in the street, kicking him. A guard ran several steps into the street from my door, leveled a shotgun at the three kickers and fired. One of them was lifted three feet back to the sidewalk. The others ran. The guard grabbed Sammy's leg and dragged him toward the door. By this time all the blacks had fled. Guards went out and pulled the dead or wounded into the buildings. Silence returned. After ten minutes it was just another hot summer's day. Serene. Except for a few smeared streaks of blood in the street.

I decided it was time to get out. I didn't mind rioters smashing into the apartment and tearing the hell out of it, but I didn't want to be there when they did it. And I sure as hell didn't want Susan to be there. So I decided to stock up the country house with food, move in with Susan, and wait for the smoke to clear.

The next morning we were packed, and I was headed for the door when the buzzer sounded.

Susan and I both froze. It was the only time in my life I had ever wished I had a gun.

The buzzer sounded again—short, polite, not too demanding. A request.

I tiptoed the two steps to the door and squinted through the peephole. I saw two white men in business suits.

"Who is it?" I called.

"Police."

"Let me see your shield."

One of them took a leather folder from his pocket, opened it, and held the shield to the peephole.

I opened the door on the chain latch.

"I'm Detective Tacker," the one with the shield said, "and this is Detective Nicholson. We have a communication for you from the Manhattan DA's office. May we come in?"

I recognized Nicholson as one of the men who'd been following me. The other, Tacker, was tall, past sixty, with white hair and a face pleasant but firm. He had a small silver pig in his button hole. It occurred to me later that he had looked knowing, as if already aware exactly how everything was going to turn out.

I unfastened the chain and let them in. They nodded politely to Susan. Tacker handed me an envelope with a note in it. The note was written on DA letterhead, signed by Steven Burk, the DA. The phrasing was Burk's too—polite, deferential, but fast, factual, no wasted words. He said the situation in the Tombs had grown "complex and critical," and unless something was done immediately "many lives would be lost." He said he understood that I was on the side of the inmates, but he also knew that I would not favor unnecessary bloodshed. Would I come to Warden Dunlop's office and listen to an assessment of the situation? I could decide then what other steps, if any, I was willing to take.

I read the note in the hall. Then I walked into the living room and sat down. Susan and the detectives followed me.

"What is it?" Susan said, looking worried.

"Just a moment," I said.

I did not want to be conned into letting myself be used as a tool by the court or city officials to mollify the inmates. On the other hand, the inmates seemed clearly to be winning now, and if I could act to reduce bloodshed without limiting their victory, I would do it. I trusted the DA. I did not think he would have written that letter unless the situation was indeed critical and unless he felt there was a good chance I could help.

I handed the letter to Susan.

"Okay," I said to Tacker. "Let's go."

Susan read the letter.

"But could you wait outside just a second," I said. "I want to—"

"Of course," Tacker said.

I let them out and closed the door. Susan handed the note back. Her face was expressionless. Alicia Bonner's face had been expressionless.

"You'll be killed," she said.

"No, I won't. Maybe I won't do anything. But I have to go and at least listen and see what the situation is. I can't just say I'm not interested and walk away."

She nodded but didn't speak.

I handed her the car keys.

"Now, listen. Get one of the lobby guards to walk you to the garage. Take the car and bags and go to the country. Fast and straight, understand? Put the car in the garage, close the garage, go in the house, and stay there. There's enough food for a few days. I'll probably be there a couple of hours after you. Don't decide to go wandering around. Don't go to the town to buy some ketchup or something. Stay there. Understand?"

"How will you get there? There won't be any bus."

"I'll get a car. Maybe these guys will take me. Or I'll steal a car. Don't worry. I'll get there. Okay? As soon as I can. Maybe sooner."

I kissed her goodby. Then I turned around, walked out the door and left her there.

■

My attorney came today with a reporter. That's strictly forbidden, he snuck him in as a member of his staff. He was a young double-breasted guy named Bonino from the *Daily News*. Fortunately I was dressed when they came. He wanted to know how I felt about the way things were turning out. As if I had any idea how they were turning out. We weren't allowed radios, the guards said nothing, and I hadn't seen my lawyer in days. "How are they turning out?" I said.

"Well, I mean—"

"The last I heard," I said, "was they had martial law in New York, they had made a few arrests."

"They've arrested about three thousand people. There've been some executions, about four we think, for killing troops."

I sat down on the edge of the bunk.

"The city's pretty quiet now," he said, as if to console me.

"Order has been restored," I said.

"More or less."

"But not law."

"I guess it depends what you call law."

"What do *you* think's going to happen?" I asked him.

"I think we'll get a civil government back in pretty soon, and the troops, most of them, will leave. I don't know what kind of a civil government. I think it will depend on what happens in other cities and in Washington. The riots there haven't been contained yet."

He asked what I thought was going to become of me.

"I guess it doesn't matter very much. If I can stay in prison until they're forced to deal with me in some legal fashion, with some due process, then I will have a chance."

I had to stop and think for a moment. The reporter and my attorney were leaning against a wall.

"My whole life has been a gradual suicide since I started this thing. It's very dangerous to tell people the truth."

He looked closely at me and then glanced around the cell. "How have you been bearing up?"

"You mean in prison, with the confinement?"

"Yes. That, and everything."

"The confinement doesn't bother me. I've always enjoyed solitude. There's an enormous amount of mediocrity in the practice of criminal law, so when you are good at it and insist on exercising your superiority, you end up pretty much alone. That's okay with me."

"Why do you think it took so long for the people to wake up?"

"About their criminal justice system? What makes you think they've woken up? What makes you think they will ever wake up? The people are like the cuckolded husband, always the last to know. Justice is relative and subjective. It is what certain people say it is at a given time. For example, we had cops, who are supposed to catch thieves, thieving. We had judges, who are supposed to be incorruptible, taking bribes. We had jail guards, who are supposed to prevent riots, rioting. It all seemed inverted, unnatural. But at the time, given the conditions, it was perfectly natural. It appeared unnatural only to someone not properly aligned. The public suffers from moral vertigo."

He looked puzzled.

"While I've got you here," I said, "let me confuse you completely. Ask me why it all happened, this sudden, violent disordering of our society."

"Okay. Why did it all happen?"

"Because true order—universal, absolute, cosmic order—is intolerable to humans. Humans are disorderly. They create civilizations, societies, structures, systems, in an attempt to achieve order. They create a system—a political system, a judicial system—in an attempt at order. But as much as humans want order, they cannot tolerate it. Humans and order are incompatible. Machines are orderly, systems are orderly. Not humans. Humans create an orderly system, but when that system grows too strong and inflexible—too orderly—human society rejects it as a body rejects foreign tissue. A system will be tolerated only so long as it is minor and unnoticed and can bend and compromise. But compromise is not in the nature of a system any more than order is in the nature of a human. As the system grows, it refuses to compromise, it draws attention to itself, it offends human disorderliness, and it is destroyed. That is what has happened. It remains only to be seen how deep the destruction goes. Does it go simply into the criminal justice system's overlying structure, or deeper into the system itself, or beyond that system into the social structure, or deeper still into the heart of our civilization? How far do you think it goes?"

The reporter glanced at my attorney, who was smiling. "I couldn't tell you."

"Neither could I."

Both of them thought I was crazy.

Well, perhaps.

EIGHT

THEY HAD a green Plymouth detective's car. A shotgun lay unobtrusively on the floor of the front seat, as unobtrusively as a shotgun ever does anything. Tacker and I sat in the back. Nicholson drove. We took the FDR Drive. It was empty.

"Anyway, it solved the traffic problem," Nicholson said. "Nothing but wrecks."

Tacker grunted.

I had the peculiar feeling I was in their custody. I wondered what their instructions had been, in the event that I refused to go with them.

We got off at the Brooklyn Bridge. A couple of blocks from the court building we passed three men with two-by-fours breaking through the glass window of a drugstore. They were the only men on the street. Nicholson kept going.

About a hundred correction officers in civilian clothes had collected on the sidewalk across the street from the Tombs entrance. Standing in ranks in the street between them and the door was a company of uniformed soldiers with helmets, gas mask bags and rifles.

"Who are they?" I said.

"National Guard," Tacker said. "Got here this morning."

So now the guards were in street clothes and someone else had the helmets and the uniforms and the gas masks.

I hadn't seen or heard about National Guard troops anywhere else in the city. The Governor and the Mayor had been fierce enemies for many years, and the Governor, who controlled the troops, had in the past few days shown no great eagerness to bail out his opponent. How ironic, I thought, that troops who could be elsewhere in the city protecting lives and property were instead here at the Tombs protecting power.

On the way into Dunlop's office I passed an Army colonel coming out. He was short, thickly built, with polished boots and starched uniform. He had a touch too much assurance, condescension even, as he nodded cordially and held the door for me.

There was nothing starched about Dunlop. He looked like an exhausted zombie. When I walked in he neither rose from his desk nor shook hands. He hadn't changed clothes or shaved since the last time I saw him. I guessed he hadn't slept much either. His eyes were red and puffed.

"The situation is this," he began hoarsely, with great fatigue, emotionless as a recorded announcement. "I guess you heard about Trouman, our PR guy, getting killed last night."

"Yes, I did."

"Well this morning the court decided to parole a couple of hundred more inmates from all the jails. Fifty from here. We sent word up to the floors for the inmates we wanted. Then we sent four officers up with gas and batons to take them to the crossover on seven, six at a time. We got thirteen men from five and ten, delivered them to court, no problems. Then the officers went to get six men on eight. Butterfield had them on the bridge ready to go. But somewhere between eight and the crossover the four officers recognized one of the inmates as an inciter in the winter riot. By the time they got off the elevator on seven the officers had turned into rioters, or mutineers I guess you'd call them. They threatened the two officers on the crossover gate and took their keys and locked them in a holding pen and left two rebel officers with them. Then the other two mutineers took the inmates down to the receiving room, threatened the two officers there with the batons and the gas, overcame them and locked them in a holding pen and put the six inmates in another holding pen. Whether or not they actually had to physically over- come these officers or whether the officers joined up with them, I'm not so sure. Sanchez, this officer named San- chez, Manuel Sanchez, who has made himself a spokes- man for the rebels, says they've got them locked up and they're hostages and he's prepared to hurt them and the inmates if he has to. Then he goes into the middle gate area out there, between the front door and the elevators— and you see he got into the middle gate easy, as easy as they got into the crossover and the receiving room, be- cause the officers there had no idea what was going on, that they were mutinying. So he got into the middle gate, and turned on the officer there with his gas and baton, and hustled him into the receiving room and they stuck him in the pen with the other officers. Or he says they did. Actually, all these officers could be joined up with them. I don't know. I do know they have the inmates locked up in the receiving room. The officers standing around in the clerical area and the entrance area outside the middle gate couldn't do anything because Sanchez was yelling that if they did anything, tried to unlock the gate or put some gas in, he'd hurt the other officers and the inmates in the receiving room. So I go out and I ask Sanchez what the fuck he thinks he's doing. We're standing there with the gate between us, just a couple of feet apart, discussing it. I haven't slept for four days, I got rioting inmates upstairs threatening to chop up my officers, and now I got officers down here with their own hostages. I think I'm gonna get me a couple of hostages myself."

He was not alone in the office. A captain and an assistant deputy warden sat in uniform beside the desk. Both men looked disheveled, unwashed and exhausted. Neither spoke, nor appeared always to be listening. In a corner on the other side of the desk sat a black man I took immediately for an inmate. His jeans, cut off at the thigh, were torn and frayed. His white T-shirt was dirty and blood-splattered. His hair, Afro style, had a comb sticking out of it. A bandage, filthy and blood-soaked, was taped to a three-inch-wide shaved furrow on the left side of his head. His face was dirty, bloody, but alert. I had no idea what he was doing in that office. The other three seemed not to notice him. It was disturbing.

"So Sanchez tells me they recognized one of the four as an inciter in the winter riot. He says they aren't gonna release him 'cause they're not gonna release no one who was taking their fellow officers hostage and getting inmates to riot and threatening them and all that. And he says they aren't gonna release no one else either. They don't like the idea of it. You see, they're startin' to see the heavy ones go now, the murderers, and they don't like that. Sanchez is from East Harlem. Sanchez knows these guys and he don't like them. He figures he made it, he worked, he got himself a good job, and all they do is steal and sell junk. A man like that don't like just bringin' 'em down on the elevator and lettin' 'em go. And he particularly don't like it if some of those men are the ones who would've taken him hostage and maybe killed him and left his family without a man. You understand? It's hard to disagree with him.

"So Sanchez and his men have the crossover and the receiving room and the elevators and now we don't have access to the floors. Except for the back fire stairs, which I get scared of when I even think about opening them. And meanwhile the rioters on the other floors want to know how come no one's coming to pick up men to go to court for parole. They say we backed down from our promise. We promised that if they'd cool things, we'd start up the paroles again. And now they think we're playing games. We tell them we've lost the elevators to rebelling officers, but they don't believe us. And you can't blame them for that either. They never heard before of officers rioting and taking hostages. So we got inmates upstairs all heated up and threatening to kill hostages and trying to get down here and storm the first floor. And on top of it all, we got the court calling and wanting to know where are the defendants. They think we're holding back. Some guy in Rhein's office calls and says our refusal to transfer inmates to court is in direct violation of the law. He says Rhein told him to tell me that he's gonna have me and anyone else responsible arrested. 'Oh, yeah?' I tell him. 'Well that's beautiful, and where you gonna lock us up?' You think we're holding back, I told him, you come over here and look yourself.

"Then we get the soldier boys outside. And if they decide to come in and take the defendants to court themselves, I won't be surprised. I'll be dead, but I won't be surprised. Because that's just what they're ready to do. That's what that colonel says they're gonna do right now. 'If those inmates aren't on their way to court in five minutes,' he tells me, 'my orders are to come in here and get them.' And Sanchez is in the middle. He's got the rioters upstairs wanting out. And he's got the court and the soldiers outside wanting in. And as soon as someone makes a move, we're gonna have a bloodbath. We'll have a riot that'll make all the other riots that ever were look like practice."

"What do you want me to do?"

"The DA and some other people are talking to Rhein right now, and the other PJs and the Governor, trying to keep them from using the soldiers to enforce their authority. I've been talking to Sanchez, trying to make him understand the position he's in and how him and a lot of other people stand to get killed. I want you to go upstairs and try to talk to Butterfield and the other leaders, to whoever's in some kind of control up there."

"How am I gonna get up? Will Sanchez let me through?"

"Sanchez will let you through. No reason not to. He wants the inmates calmed down too. But that's not the right question." He looked at me and waited.

"What's the right question?"

"How do you get out?"

"Oh, wonderful."

"I'm not gonna kid you. Getting out could be a problem. We have no idea what things are like up there, but from all I can tell it's a madhouse. We don't know for sure who the leaders are now, or if they've still got any. Every time I get someone on the phone, someone else grabs it away from him. Probably they've got more generals than the Congolese Army. We've got to get someone up there who can tell them the problem down here with Sanchez and the soldiers and make them cool things for a while until something works out. If they break through to the fire stairs or through the outer walls, it will—" He rubbed his eyes. "It will— I—"

I didn't know if he was going to cry or pass out. I did know that I wanted very badly not to go back upstairs. I am not a brave man and make no claims to bravery. If cowardice is required to preserve my life, then I'll be a coward. I should not have come here. I should be in my car driving to the country with Susan.

"Warden, I don't want to see anyone get killed. I don't want any kind of a bloodbath or anything like that. But I don't see what I could do up there. I don't know any of these men. I know Butterfield. But he may not even be in control anymore. I wouldn't know what to do when I got there. And I don't see why they should listen to anything I said."

"They know who you are."

It was the black man in the corner.

"They trust you as much as they trust any white man,

215

and they need information. They want to know what's happening down here as much as we want to know what's happening up there. I can find the leaders for you."

His voice was strong, straightforward. He knew what he had to do, and one of the things he had to do was encourage the timid.

"This is Detective Jackson," the warden said. "He's been undercover in the Tombs six weeks locating these guys, making friends."

Dunlop stopped talking. He seemed simply to run out of gas. I thought he might fall asleep. Then he started up again. "When things began getting hot, the PD told us he was here and asked us to get him out. He'd had a problem with an officer who landed a baton on him. He was one of the names we sent up for court this morning so the inmates think he came out for court. He can go back up as your escort. He'll try to look out for you and he says he can get you with the leaders."

I looked at Jackson. What kind of a man was this? And Dunlop? There was simply no way I could say no and get up and walk out of that office.

"Well," I said, "let's go then."

So again I was riding up in an elevator, smelling the stink and hearing the noise, stronger and louder as we rose. But I was not prepared for what happened when we got to eight and the doors opened. Naked, wild, sweat-covered men crashed into the open elevator as if sprayed at it from a hose. They fell down around us and more pushed in—arms, legs and bodies piling up. I was knocked to my knees, and Jackson grabbed my arms with both hands and lifted me and threw me forward on top of the bodies, fighting his way behind me. He put an arm around my waist and led and pulled me away from the elevators to the bridge.

All the gates were open, all the cells unlocked. Men ran through the open sections and the bridge, some in terror as if pursued, others laughing hysterically, waving their arms. An old man with long gray hair stood wrapped in a sheet on top of a table, screaming at the ceiling. Two young Puerto Ricans cringed together on the top bunk of an open cell. Inmates lay unconscious on the tile floors, unnoticed even by running men who tripped and stumbled on them.

We headed through A section toward the back of the floor and the fire gate. I searched through the crowding faces for Butterfield, for the hostages. I saw no one. At the fire gate, four blacks pounded on the gate frame with table legs, trying to break through bolts embedded in the concrete walls and ceiling. One of the men spotted Jackson, looked quickly from him to me, and stopped pounding.

"What you doin' back here?" he said to Jackson.

"Brought you a messenger," Jackson said. "Man who started this thing, wants to talk to you."

"Talk."

He was not what you'd call warmly familiar, but on the other hand he hadn't brained me with the table leg.

I told him about Sanchez and the National Guard troops. He listened blankly with the table leg in his hand. Then he glanced at Jackson and without a word went back to banging on the gate. He was not, as Jackson had promised, eager for my information.

Jackson took me through the floor, section by section, looking for other leaders. Many men were unconscious on the floor, some badly beaten. I was struck over and over again by the looks of pure terror on some faces and the hysterical delight on others. We found one supremely calm white man leaning casually on the open gate of C section, watching the chaos as one watches a thunderstorm through the window, having nothing else to do. He nodded pleasantly to Jackson, shook hands, and said something I couldn't hear.

"Tell him," Jackson said to me.

I moved closer to the man and he leaned his ear toward me. I told him about Sanchez and the troops. He nodded as I spoke, but never looked at me. When I was finished, he looked at Jackson and nodded and said something affirmative, as if Jackson had told him I had a good story to tell and now, having heard it, he felt obliged to comment. Then Jackson spoke to him, explaining, pleading perhaps—I could only hear fragments. The man shrugged. He was detached and unconcerned.

As I watched and tried to listen, I understood what this man knew. I realized how right he was. The six hundred inmates on this floor, and no doubt on the other floors as well, were beyond leadership or cooling off. News of troops and impending destruction was irrelevant. News of the end of the world would have been irrelevant. Nothing would have any influence now but violence.

I was facing Jackson and the white man, with my back to the elevators. For the past three or four minutes, sharp but distant banging noises had penetrated the general roar around me. I had not recognized them as gunshots.

Something in Jackson's eyes now made me turn. I saw one or two brown helmets bobbing above a mass of struggling inmates around the elevators. Then several more, then ten or fifteen.

Jackson and I left the other man and moved toward the helmets. The distant explosions continued. Soldiers pushed through the crowd with rifles, flak vests and gas masks. Men closest to the elevators were coughing. I could smell the gas. Another elevator arrived with more soldiers. Inmates jammed into it and the doors closed. Indicator lights over the elevators showed all four in action.

The soldiers pushed and fought their way to the fire gate. They unlocked it and inmates poured through, fighting and screaming.

Jackson and I went with them, swept along through the gate and down the stairs. The next flight down, soldiers held the mob back and unlocked gates. On each landing another gate blocked the stairs. The mob grew thicker and thicker on every floor as more prisoners flooded in.

I lost Jackson, but he could not have helped me. I was not afraid of anyone harming me intentionally, for the inmates' only concern was to get down the stairs. But in the crush and struggle and downward flow, men stumbled and fell and disappeared. We were a hot, oozing flow of human lava. I clung to whatever sweaty limb was close and steady.

As we descended, the smell of gas grew stronger. Men coughed, tears flooded cheeks. Finally I saw the bottom. Then I was at the bottom gate, and shot through it like a popped cork into the receiving room.

Gas and gunsmoke filled my eyes and lungs. I pulled my shirt over my face, closed my eyes and tried not to breathe. I followed the mob. I stepped on something soft, took two more steps and stumbled. The mob stopped moving. I had to breathe. I was falling. I was going to die here. I clutched at the man in front of me. He gave way and fell. I felt hands on my back, pushing. The mob moved again. I stumbled, crawled and fell forward into a sudden fresh coolness. The middle gate. I could see the front door open. Air rushed in. Short breaths burned but were possible. Finally I was through the middle gate and breathing by the door. Inmates swarmed into the street. Soldiers in gas masks pulled and dragged men through the middle gate to the entrance hall. I leaned against the wall by the door and breathed. I didn't want to fight the mob to get through that door. I just wanted to be allowed the cool fresh breaths of air that came in past me over their heads.

I stood there leaning my weight against the wall for five or ten minutes. I thought about Oscar. Probably the first one out. By now he's back in Harlem dealing ounces. Then I slumped down and sat on the floor and put my face in my hands. I felt something sticky on my face and pulled my head up and looked at my hands. They were covered with blood. I had crawled through it. The floor around me was streaked with red smears where bodies had been dragged from the receiving room and middle gate. I saw eight bodies stretched along the wall with flak jackets over their heads. Some had khaki uniforms, some blue. I stood up and looked around. The edges of the wall were lined with bodies, thirty or forty of them, some places two deep, dragged from beneath the trampling feet, covered with flak jackets. In the back of the clerical section toward Dunlop's office I saw more bodies, plasma bottles raised over them, soldiers bending.

I looked around for Dunlop. All I saw were soldiers and inmates. I asked soldiers if they'd seen the warden. They ignored me. Then one of their officers said, "He's dead." That's all. He was headed into the middle gate and didn't have time to stop.

I pushed into the mob at the door and squeezed through to the street. Army ambulances filled the block. Guards and police, black and white, some in uniform, chased running inmates with two-by-fours and baseball bats. Soldiers ran back and forth breaking up fights. I edged along the side of the building, breathing lungs full of air, feeling the breeze cool my eyes, trying to get out of the crowd to safety.

"Mr. Dori."

Tacker had come up behind me. He had a hand on my shoulder. "Over here."

He moved ahead of me toward the back of the court building, toward Carlo's. I saw Nicholson now, too, following behind us.

I was astonished to find Carlo's open and doing business as usual. Men filled the tables and crowded the bar. There's no killing commerce.

"What'll you have?" Tacker said.

"Dewars rocks."

Tacker leaned through the crowd at the bar, put down a twenty-dollar bill and ordered the drinks.

Someone moved off a stool and Nicholson said, "Sit down."

"That's okay. You take it." I wanted to go back to the men's room and wash my hands.

"Sit down," Tacker said, handing me the Scotch. "You need a rest."

Something in his tone made me accept the drink. I settled myself on the stool and took a long sip. I had never tasted anything so cold and beautiful. I looked up, and Tacker and Nicholson were staring at me. I had the same feeling I'd had in the car, that I was in their custody. What did they think they were protecting me from, or saving me for?

"Some court," Nicholson said.

"What?"

"Some court." This time he nodded toward the street.

"What do you mean?"

"They had a judge out there, and lawyers. He was the first to go."

Of course. They wouldn't want to release the inmates without some procedure. Even in defeat they grasped at form.

"Who?" I asked.

"Malizard."

Nicholson was studying my reaction. The whole feeling in the bar was exceptionally bizarre. Driving down to the Tombs, the streets had been empty, but this bar was packed. Even the jukebox roared, Frank Sinatra singing love songs as if nothing had happened. Men pushed in so close around me I had to lean forward and backward to let them reach in for their drinks. They stared at me, aware who I was, and kept an eye on Tacker and Nicholson.

A heavyset man in a yellow sport shirt came up and said hello to Tacker.

"Big crowd," Tacker said.

"When they heard about the trouble everyone came down to see if they could help," the man said.

Then he looked at me.

"Mr. Dori," he said, but did not put out his hand. He wanted to be sure I knew that he knew who I was.

"Just come out?" he said. He was civil, but he had a lot he wanted to say.

"Yeah."

Tacker and Nicholson were spectators.

"I hear a lot of people got hurt," the man said, looking at my hands.

"That's right."

"These guys had a lot of friends in there."

"I know."

He looked at me a long time, then turned to Tacker and Nicholson, said, "See you," and moved away.

Now other men started talking to me. A lot of them recognized me, had seen me in court. The hostility was undisguised. How did I feel about the men who'd been killed? Did I know they were friends of the men in the bar? Did I know they had wives and children? Did I think conditions were better now than they had been? Why did I start all this? Why was I only thinking about the defendants, what about the correction officers and the cops and the citizens?

I used the word "guard" once and was corrected instantly. I tried to remember to say correction officer. More men pushed in around me to interrogate me. They leaned, crowded, jostled. Serious answers were impossible. I said whatever I thought might conciliate.

I wanted to leave, but was afraid to try. I didn't want to test these men's intentions. Everytime I shifted position on the stool I sensed or imagined a corresponding, matching move in the bodies surrounding me. If I tried to leave and was blocked, I would panic.

Tacker had disappeared. Nicholson watched and listened.

I wanted more than ever to get the blood off my hands, and I had to go to the bathroom. I decided to move slowly off the bar stool and walk toward the men's room, not toward the door, and see what happened. It was a compromise.

Nothing happened. The crowd separated to allow my passage. I must be paranoid, I thought. No one wants to hurt me.

Still, when I got in the men's room and saw the window, I didn't hesitate. I forgot about my hands and going to the bathroom. I fastened the door with a hook-and-eye latch and climbed up on the sink beneath the window. I was kneeling on top of the sink, pulling the screen out, when the toilet stall door opened.

It was Tacker.

"What the hell are you doing up there?"

"I'm trying to get out of this fucking place."

"Well if you want to leave, say so. Come on."

He could not have been nicer, one of those pleasant men who have heard the last word, life's punch line, and age thenceforth into a bemused and quiet wisdom. He helped me down from the sink, flipped open the door latch, and followed me out. He picked his change off the bar, leaving two dollars, and the three of us walked out.

It was nine o'clock, dark.

"Where can we take you?" Tacker said. We were in the back seat again, me behind Nicholson.

I wanted to go to the country, but not with them.

"The apartment," I said, "if you don't mind."

We turned left on Canal Street and drove crosstown. My apartment was uptown. I said nothing.

"You're not in a hurry, are you, Allan?"

It was Nicholson, calling me Allan.

"Why?"

"We'd like to take a look around. If you're not in a hurry."

"Why not?"

I tried to think things out. Why would these men want to hurt me? For a lot of reasons. They blamed me in general for this whole mess, for the disruption and endangerment of their lives, and they blamed me in particular for the deaths of their friends. The cops and guards hated me because they thought I was on the side of the defendants. The defendants hated me because they thought I was on the side of the authorities. Rhein and the Mayor and that bunch hated me because they thought I was on the side of criminals. No one thought I was on the side of justice. You can't be on the side of anything as abstract as justice. You can only be on the side of people.

"Law squad," Nicholson said, slowing down.

"And troops," Tacker said.

We were in Sheridan Square, Greenwich Village. Three bodies lay in front of the smashed window of a bank. Two men fired shots from behind a car parked in front of the bank. Another group returned the fire from the corner of a building near where we had stopped. In the middle of the square, machine-gun fire exploded from an armored personnel carrier.

Nicholson spun the wheel and stepped on the gas. We

went up on the sidewalk, back to the street, and took off down Seventh Avenue.

"Are you working or striking or what?" I said.

"I guess we're working. Are we working, Tacker?"

"We're working," Tacker said. "They're still a few of us good guys left. Fighting crime."

We drove all over the city. The Battery, Wall Street, Fifth Avenue. Fifth Avenue was wrecked, every window broken. Men darted like rats through the darkness. I heard pistol shots and occasional bursts of machine-gun fire. Another armored personnel carrier churned by in the opposite direction. A jeep followed us for a block, but Nicholson speeded up, made a fast turn toward Madison, and we lost it.

Tacker grew silent. Nicholson spoke. He admired Tacker greatly, but obviously thought admiration too bold an admission of inferiority and tried to hide it. That meant making a show of doing things his own way.

"Let's go see the boys at Manhattan North," he said to Tacker. "Maybe someone's at the house."

That shot fear through me. I was determined not to get trapped inside a station house full of rebelling cops.

"I'd like to get back to the apartment," I said.

"Just two minutes," Nicholson said. "Make a fast check."

"Why not?" Tacker said quietly. His mind seemed somewhere else.

"Listen," I said, "I've been gassed today, I've been threatened, I damned near died today. I want to get home."

"Couple of minutes," Nicholson said.

I looked at Tacker. Nothing. He was so detached, knowing, a man watching a movie he's already seen. I wondered if he'd been in the men's room waiting for me. He hadn't acted all that surprised to find me on the sink.

"What are you doing?" I said to both of them.

No answer.

"Stop playing games with me. If there's something you want, tell me."

No answer.

"What are you going to do?"

"He's right," Tacker said finally. "I'm getting tired myself. Go through the park."

My stomach dropped. Fear is when you anticipate an unpleasant event, terror is when you await it. Tacker's words turned my fear to terror.

We were on Fifth Avenue in the sixties, passing the apartment house I lived in when I was a child, passing the zoo. At 72nd Street, Nicholson made a left into the transverse cutting through Central Park to the West Side. The park was an empty black hole, never more menacing.

"What are you going to do?"

Silence.

Then Tacker said, firmly but with no malice, quite nicely, in fact, "We're government employees, Mr. Dori. We're peace officers. We do what the government tells us to do, to keep the peace."

We were passing Army tents, some kind of stockade, barbed wire and sentries and lights. A bus with wire mesh over the windows was unloading civilians.

"Fill 'er up," Nicholson shouted. "Pack 'em in! Pack 'em in!"

"Some of them are cops," Tacker said quietly.

We came out of the park and turned right on Broadway. I heard a loud crack and the car lurched.

Nicholson speeded up. The hood had a dent in it. We were doing eighty.

I tried to hold the terror down, and think. They could be taking me to New Jersey, or to the river, or they could turn back into the park.

"Go with it," Tacker said suddenly.

Nicholson didn't answer, but his eyes were on the rear view mirror. We had a car behind us, almost touching the bumper.

I met Nicholson's eyes in the mirror.

"You can get out here, Allan," he said. We were going over sixty.

"What do you think?" Tacker said.

"Let's try 'em," Nicholson said.

Nicholson pulled to the right and slowed down. The car behind us came up alongside.

Then I understood. Television two nights ago had had something about a new technique in mugging. They called it auto-mugging.

Nicholson kept slowing down and gave the other car an angry, frightened wave. The other car pulled in front and stopped. Nicholson stopped and shifted into reverse.

A black man with a gun walked back to Nicholson's window. Another black man was getting out the driver's side.

The man with the gun gestured for Nicholson to roll his window down. Nicholson obeyed. Tacker leaned across me and rolled down my window. The man came up to Nicholson and said something.

"What?" Nicholson said.

"Out of the car," the man said.

"What?" Tacker said from the back seat, practically in my lap now.

The man pushed the gun through the window at Nicholson and started to speak. Nicholson grabbed his arm and wrist with both hands and stepped on the gas.

The car jumped back. I was thrown to the floor with Tacker. I felt us speeding backward.

"Get the wheel!" Tacker yelled, scrambling back to the seat.

I came up off the floor and saw a black hand with a gun in it bent over the back of the seat. Tacker clutched the hand. The man's head was in Nicholson's chest.

Nicholson stopped the car and slammed it into a forward gear. Tacker twisted the man's wrist back until the gun dropped. I heard a bone crack.

"Don't move, motherfucker," Tacker said.

Nicholson shot the car forward. His lights picked up the other mugger, motionless as a stunned rabbit. The man began to run, too late.

I put my head down and felt a jolt and heard a bang and a thud. I looked up and saw the man on the hood. Nicholson jammed on the brakes and the man kept going, shooting forward into the street ahead of us. Nicholson hit the gas again and the car lurched forward over the body. When we got up to fifty, Tacker let go of the first man's arm. Nicholson took his right hand off the wheel and gave the top of the man's head a hard shove toward the window, as if jamming it into a bag.

The man yelled "No!" and was gone.

Tacker turned and looked out the rear window. Then he picked the gun off the floor and tossed it out.

We were headed up Broadway. No one spoke.

Then Nicholson looked down at his chest. "Bastard puked all over my shirt."

Tacker was back in his trance.

Up ahead at 96th Street a car was on its side burning. Nicholson slowed down to forty. Tacker said, "Let's have a look. Take it easy."

We slowed almost to a stop in front of the car, and started slowly around it.

"Empty," Nicholson said, and started speeding up. It was my only chance. I pushed open the door and jumped.

"Thanks for gettin' us all out," Ajax said.

"Yeah," I said.

I didn't want to stay up there all night with Ajax and those other madmen. I had to get to the country. What had become of Susan?

"Listen," I said, wondering how far Ajax's gratitude went. "I need a car."

"You got it. Gimme ten minutes."

He looked like he wasn't all that unhappy to see me getting out of there.

He left, and I sat on the floor and pretended to be absorbed in the TV set. Someone was interviewing someone in a studio. The sound was off. The two men watched with concentration, but no one turned the sound up.

Ajax came back and took me down to the street and a white '73 Mustang. "Sorry about the color. They ain't too many left still workin'."

"Thanks a lot, Ajax. You've saved my life."

He said nothing. We shook hands.

Two hours later I turned off into the dirt road to my house. I drove slowly with the parking lights, searching the road and shoulders. I don't know what I expected to find. If I gained anything in the past twenty-four hours it was caution.

I didn't see my car, but the garage door was closed. I hoped it was in there. No lights showed in the house. Ever since I'd left Ajax and had had time to think, I'd been desperate to be with Susan. Tomorrow or the next day when the Army had things under control we'd drive to an airport and fly the hell out of there, out of the country, to the Caribbean or Hawaii or the Mediterranean. We'd travel and be happy.

I saw no sign of her. I told myself the car was in the garage.

I parked in the road and got out quietly, not closing the door. I walked over to the garage and lifted the latch and let the door swing open six inches.

The garage was empty.

I'd had enough. The Tombs, gas, Nicholson, Tacker. I didn't even feel the fear anymore. I loved Susan and if I lost her I was going to lose something I didn't have much of left.

I walked over to the house and unlocked the door and went in. I wasn't even trying to be quiet. If anyone wanted to hurt me, they could fucking well go ahead.

"Allan!"

Susan threw herself at me and went limp in my arms. I almost collapsed with fright. She lifted her head and tried to talk. Nothing came through.

"It's all right," I said. "It's all right. Everything's all right."

I stood holding her for a long moment, then helped her over to the sofa and sat down.

"I thought . . . I thought it was . . ."

"It's all right, Susan. Don't try to talk. Everything's okay now."

It was ten minutes before she could tell me what had happened. Two cars had followed her all the way to the country. She said she'd had the Porsche up to 120 and they stayed with her. She'd been afraid to make the turnoff to the house and show them where it was, so she kept going and slowed down and drove the car off the road into the woods. She ran into the woods and heard the other cars stop and someone yell, "She's in the trees!" She ran through the woods for thirty minutes to the house and had been sitting there on the sofa for eight hours.

"I heard you and I was sure it was them. I wanted you so bad, Allan. I was sure you were dead. When I heard someone outside I knew it was them. I heard someone at the garage and then banging in the front door and I knew it was them."

We sat there for an hour until she calmed down. Then I turned on the TV. Nothing but snow, not even test patterns. I went upstairs for a portable transistor radio in the bedroom and brought it down. An announcer on WNBC said the TV stations were off the air and NBC Radio would be broadcasting straight uninterrupted news. He said riots had broken out in Philadelphia, Washington and Detroit. Then he played an announcement taped by the Mayor two hours earlier. "We are appealing to the leaders of these disturbances to show their good faith and abide by the agreements reached at the time of their release. We have every belief that they will do so."

The station switched to a reporter on top of the RCA Building, in the Rainbow Room of all places, describing his view of New York. Large sections of the city were blacked out in power failures. Harlem, Bedford-Stuyvesant, Williamsburg and the South Bronx were almost totally in flames. His voice was calm, but not detached. You could hear the emotion. He sounded like Edward R. Murrow describing the blitz from a London rooftop.

I took Susan by the hand and we went upstairs with the radio onto the roof. We stood there on the grass in a cool breeze. Edward R. Murrow was still describing New York.

"You can see it," Susan said.

The southern sky reflected the faint pink glow of fire, like the beginning of a sunrise. What pride a revolutionary would have taken in that sight. I felt lonely and desperate.

"Still feel like throwing bombs?" I said.

"Who needs bombs?"

"When you've got a bastard like me."

"I didn't mean that. I meant that it blew up by itself, without bombs."

"Are you pleased?"

There was a long silence. Then she said, "Yes."

Suddenly the radio went off. Nothing but static. We stood there silently in the dark, looking south. We listened to the static and watched the sunrise. New York.

I heard a noise.

"Stay here," I said.

The noise had come from the front of the house facing the garage. I tiptoed downstairs and looked out a window by the porch. A man was in the yard, moving toward the front door. It was Fischer.

I opened the door. "Dave—"

He came in quickly and closed the door. "Sorry to bother you, Allan. I gotta talk to you."

"Just a minute."

I took him up to the roof.

Susan was astonished to see him. "What are you doing here?"

"Terrorizing the countryside."

"Don't try to be funny."

"What are you doing on the roof?"

"Look," Susan said, pointing south.

"I—is that New York?"

"That's it," Susan said.

Fischer stared. Then he said, "Can't you get a station on that thing?"

"They went off the air," I said.

"Listen," Fischer said, "I've got to talk to you."

We went down to the living room.

"There's about a million warrants out for you, Allan. State and federal."

"What for?"

"Inciting to riot. Conspiracy to commit murder. Conspiracy to commit arson. Conspiracy to destroy the whole fucking world. You'd better get moving, man."

I was on the sofa next to Susan. We were in the dark. For all I knew the power was off. The radio had said telephone service was suspended at midnight. It was 2 A.M.

"There's something else, Allan. In case you're wondering about whether you ought to run or not."

He was across from us on a cushion on the floor.

"What's that?"

"There're some people looking for you who don't care about the warrants."

"What does that mean?" Susan said, sitting forward.

"Allan . . ."

"What does it mean?" she said.

"Some people think you're head of a conspiracy to overthrow the government. They think it was all planned out with the black groups. They think you're head of some organization. They want to kill you."

Susan slumped back.

"They're on their way, Allan. I got out ahead of them by maybe half an hour. You'd better move."

"You got out of where?" I said. "Ahead of whom?"

"Carlo's. Cops. And some people I wasn't sure about. They looked like federal people, Army or Justice Department. I don't know. There were a couple of guys I never saw before doing a lot of talking. They could have been from anywhere. But they knew what they were doing. It'll be a lynching, Allan. If I could—"

A light flashed on the porch.

Fischer stopped talking.

We listened.

Footsteps outside the door. I looked at Fischer and saw a gun in his hand.

A knock. Then another—louder, banging.

"Police! Open the door!"

Fischer stood up. Susan and I tiptoed toward him, toward the gun.

"I'm the police!" Fischer called. "I'm an assis—"

"Are you armed?"

Fischer glanced at me. New York police always take great interest in the identity of other lawmen. This guy didn't sound like a New Yorker.

"No," Fischer said, and put the pistol in his trouser pocket.

We waited.

Gunshots exploded on the porch. Pencil-sized splinters of wood flew at us from the door. Three men charged in with flashlights.

The first man swept his light quickly around the room and pushed a gun toward Fischer.

"Who are you?" he shouted. The light trembled.

Fischer had his shield out. "David Fischer, Assistant DA. Manhattan."

The light jumped to Susan. "You!"

"Susan Bernfeld. I'm an attorney."

The light hit me.

"You're Dori!"

"That's right."

I squinted into the light. The man had a striped shirt. I could hardly make out the others. They might have been unarmed.

"Come out here," the man said to me.

"Just—" Fischer started. The man jabbed the gun at him, then moved cautiously aside to let me get to the door.

"Wait a minute," Fischer said. "Who the hell—"

The man's other hand flicked forward like a snake's tongue and his flashlight struck Fischer hard in the chest, pushing him back two steps to the wall.

The man looked at me and waved his light in the direction of the door. "Out!"

If I went out, I was dead. If I didn't go out, I was dead —and probably Susan and Fischer with me. I decided to follow orders. I started to move. Then I saw Fischer's hand climb slowly toward his pocket.

I heard shots.

I heard Susan yell, "Shoot!"

Beyond that my memory loses motion. I recall only three stationary images: a flash of light illuminating Fischer's arm, his hand gripping the gun, slender brown fingers tight on black steel; Susan's head thrown straight back, pivoting on the neck, mouth open, eyes filled with shock; the face of the man in the striped shirt, jaws tense, lips pressed hard together, eyes wide—that last trigger-pulling, moral-thin increment of brutal resolve.

Then I was looking up from an operating table into lights and faces. A man's voice said, "Demerol," and I passed out.

I kept coming to and passing out for two days. I was still at the farm with Susan. We were outside by the fire making love. We were on the roof watching the red glow in the sky. We were inside listening to Fischer. She never stopped looking at me, never stopped touching me.

When I was conscious long enough to assemble my thoughts, I started asking about her. The doctors and nurses kept saying, "Quiet, now. Just rest, now. Everything's fine." It was two days before I got an answer. An old attorney friend of mine came in the room and said he was representing me.

"Where's Susan?" I said.

"Dead, Allan. I'm—"

"Fischer?"

"Fischer too. I'm sorry, Allan. We found the gun outside in a ditch with prints on it. He'll be brought to justice, Allan."

To justice. "By God then," I said. "But by no one else. Not on this earth."

These are some smart sons of bitches. This morning, when the new tour of guards came on, they were men I'd never seen before.

I said to one, "Where are the other officers?"

"What other officers?"

"The ones who're usually here."

"They've been transferred."

"Where?"

"To a prison."

"This *is* a prison."

"Not anymore."

"What is it?"

"A mental hospital."

I started screaming.

The psychiatrist came in, the cadaver.

"What the hell's going on?" I yelled at him.

"Calm down. There's nothing to be alarmed about."

"Tell me what the hell's going on!"

"The state needed another medical facility, so this institution was designated. That's all. Nothing to get excited about."

"You mean I'm in a mental hospital, a fucking *asylum*?"

"You are in a state mental hospital."

I collapsed onto the bunk. "Oh, what the hell are you going to do to me *now*?"

"Mr. Dori, we are not going to do anything *to* you. We are going to do things *for* you. We are going to help you."